SOMETHING LIKE HATE

CHICAGO GRIZZLIES

PIPER RAYNE

ABOUT SOMETHING LIKE HATE

I love him.

I loathe him

It's like plucking daisy petals in my head, but he'll never know.

When Miles Cavanaugh, the best safety in the league, was traded to the Chicago Grizzlies football team last year, I could finally breathe. Temptation was miles away.

How naïve to think it would end there because when the opportunity to write for a national magazine based in Chicago lands in my lap months later, I can't turn it down. Sure, it's a big city, but the sexual energy feels like a beacon between us the minute my plane lands.

To make matters worse, I end up having to take over the job of reporting exclusively on the Chicago Grizzlies. Which means traveling with the team, interviewing players, and pretty much having an all-access pass to their lives during the season.

Miles and I put up a great front, quickly hating on one another, but we both know it's a lie. We also know the rules are simple. For me, don't sleep with the subject of your articles. For him, don't sleep with the journalist who can make or break your career.

I thought straight-laced Miles Cavanaugh followed all the rules… oh how wrong I was.

SOMETHING
LIKE Hate

CHAPTER 1

MILES

What a great morning.

My little sister Twyla, and my old teammate Chase, who are now a couple, are visiting from San Francisco and staying with me in Chicago. It feels good to have people I know so well in a city that still feels a little strange to me even though I was traded mid-season last year. It probably didn't help that last year, I flew back to San Francisco every chance I got and spent most of the off-season there. But I promised myself a fresh start this year, which means I sold my place out west and am committed to really settling in here in Chicago.

Twyla and Chase just told me they're expecting a baby. I'm going to be an uncle. I couldn't be happier for them and I'm excited for my new role, even if there's a tug of disappointment because I'll be thousands of miles away from my new niece or nephew. All the what-ifs race through my brain for the millionth time. What could I have done to avoid being traded from the team I'd been on since I was drafted? The place where all my friends are and where I'd made a life.

I'm stuck in my head—like usual these days—when my sister announces, "I have to pop out and meet someone."

My forehead creases. Who the hell does she know in Chicago besides me? Something feels off. She's looking at Chase as if she needs his support.

"I was wondering why you were already dressed and ready to go. Who are you meeting?" I ask.

"Um…I'm just going to help someone with something for the day."

I frown at her vagueness. It will be nice to spend time with Chase without watching his hands roam all over my sister, but I only have a little time left with both of them before they leave. Chase and I both have to report to our respective training camps soon.

"I didn't realize you knew anyone in Chicago. Except for me."

"Well… I didn't. They're new here too."

Chase chuckles, and my gaze flies over to him. "Just tell him, sunshine."

I still. "Tell me what?"

My sister shifts in place and her eyes lock with mine. "Bryce got a job at *Sportsverse Magazine,* and their head office is here in Chicago, so she just moved here. I'm helping her unpack and get organized at her new place." She rambles it out so fast that it's like she's hoping I won't catch the keywords. Bryce. *Sportsverse.* Chicago. Move. New place.

I blink as each word repeats in my head until I find the words to question whether I heard her right. "Bryce lives in Chicago now?"

She nods. "Yep. But it's a big city. I'm sure you guys won't even see each other." She gives me an encouraging smile.

I can't seem to speak a word, much less a sentence. Why would Bryce accept a position at *Sportsverse,* knowing I'm here? She hates me. I hate her. If I find out she's reporting on the Chicago Grizzlies, I might just lose my shit. Fuck, I'll retire before I let her write one more shitty word about me.

"Miles, say something," Twyla pleads.

I look between her and Chase. Both of their faces are etched in concern. I glance at her stomach… she doesn't need my stress on her shoulders, and that's exactly what will happen if I voice how I really feel about this, because Twyla would try to make it all okay. It's not her problem to worry about.

So I man up and tell Twyla what she wants to hear. "You're right, it's a big city. I'll never even see her. It's not gonna be a problem."

"Oh, I hoped you'd realize that. She doesn't even live by you. She lives down in Lakeview or something."

"What is she doing for *Sportsverse*?" I ask, trying to appear interested and not worried that she's going to be the sports reporter for the Grizzlies football team.

One reason I hate Bryce is what she did to me when I played for the San Francisco Kingsmen and she was writing for the *San Jose Chronicle*. Some might blame her for my trade, for always pointing out my flaws and focusing only on them.

There's another reason I hate her, but I try not to think of that.

"Um…I'm not sure. I never asked." Twyla kisses Chase on the cheek. "But I gotta go. Promised I'd be there by ten."

"No lifting anything heavy," Chase says.

A better man than me would suggest that Chase and I go over to help. I'd find out where Bryce lives and make damn sure never to set foot in that neighborhood again. But fuck if I'm going to help Bryce after everything that went down between us.

"I told her I'd organize her stuff as she unpacks. I'll see you guys later." She kisses Chase again and hugs me before she's out the door.

Once she's gone, Chase shoves his hands in his pockets and stares at me. "Do you want to talk about it?"

"Hell no." I walk over to my fridge, wondering if it's too early to start drinking.

"Good. Felt I had to ask though." He heads into the adjoining living room and sits on the couch, props his feet up on the table, and turns on the sports channel.

The hosts are talking about their picks for football season this year and who they think will make it to the Big Game. I groan, sitting on the chair adjacent to Chase.

He doesn't rub it in when the hosts talk about how the San Francisco Kingsmen are the reigning champs. How they might have another unstoppable team this year. Although the commentators don't remark about my trade specifically, it stings that the Kingsmen won the Big Game without me. It hurts to think that I might've let them down and held them back when I was on the team. The belief that maybe I'm just not good enough is like a bruise that refuses to heal.

"Let's talk about Cooper Rice and the Chicago Grizzlies. With Miles Cavanaugh joining them last season, I saw some potential," Rip Klein says on the TV.

"Are you suggesting Miles Cavanaugh could be a game-changer for them this season?" Ollie Pradham asks in a tone that suggests Rip Klein doesn't know what he's talking about.

Chase doesn't say much as the two of them go back and forth. Rip's on my side and Ollie's not. The only real consensus they have is that Cooper Rice is the image of professional football right now—not necessarily for his talent, but his good looks and all the endorsement deals he's done in the past year.

We sit in silence as the show goes to commercial.

"You don't believe that bullshit, do you?" Chase asks without making eye contact with me.

"No," I say, but when people constantly underestimate you, it's hard not to believe they may be onto something. Hell, Ollie Pradham is in the Hall of Fame. He was one of the best cornerbacks ever.

"Good. Because they don't know shit."

I nod, but in my head, I harp on the fact he's still a Kingsman. Chase still plays for the team I want to play for. I'm the one who got booted off the island, not him, so it's easy for him to say.

He stands and looks at me. "Let's go do something."

"Like what?" We did all the tourist stuff already.

"I don't give a shit. Anything. We just need to get the hell out of here."

I shrug. "Let's go then."

We leave the condo in search of something to do. I can push aside all the bullshit until training camp next week because that's when the vultures will come out to pick apart my performance as though I'm roadkill.

CHAPTER 2

BRYCE

"Thanks for all your help." I hug Twlya goodbye.

She'll go back to San Francisco with her boyfriend, Chase, in a couple days, after spending more time with her brother, Miles, who I cannot stand.

"You're welcome. I'm so happy for you."

"Make sure you tell Chase that I didn't work you too hard and didn't allow you to lift anything."

I cannot believe they're going to have a baby. Twyla is a little younger than me, and I'm not anywhere close to wanting to even think of starting a family.

She laughs. "He's not the boss of me."

Then we laugh together because, although Chase isn't the boss of her, he is a very big, very protective tight end for the Kingsmen.

My buzzer dings, so I press the button to answer the door in the lobby.

"Open up, Coop is about to drop the pizza. He's been complaining about how hot the bottom of the box is for the last block," my college friend Elle, says through the speaker.

I laugh and press the button. Twyla gives me a frown.

"What?"

"I'm jealous." Her frown deepens.

"Jealous?"

"We're going to miss you."

I can't deny that I love my girlfriends back in San Francisco. Although they're all married, engaged, or having a baby with a Kingsmen football player, and I do often feel like the odd woman out, I'm going to miss everyone too.

"I'm going to visit, and you guys are always welcome here. When the Kingsmen play the Grizzlies, we're definitely meeting up."

Twyla smiles. "Definitely."

I open the door in anticipation of Coop and Elle's arrival, and I can hear my two college friends arguing as they round the final set of stairs to my apartment.

"Jesus, you couldn't find a place with an elevator?" Cooper complains.

"Some of us don't make millions of dollars," Elle says. "He's been complaining since he picked me up. The pizza boxes were too hot, his legs hurt from climbing the stairs. Anything else upsetting you, Goldilocks?"

Twyla and I laugh.

"First of all, these hands are worth the millions. And it was leg day, so I'm sore." Cooper shakes his head.

"Are those hands worth millions to women or to the Grizzlies?" Elle asks.

"Oh, they're fun," Twyla says to me with a smile.

Elle and Coop stop outside my door. I take the pizza box from Coop and set it on top of a box I've yet to unpack near the door. He shakes out his hands as if it was filled with coals.

"They are fun, but they argue all the time," I whisper loudly so they can hear me.

"No, we don't," Elle says.

"Not at all," Coop adds.

I roll my eyes and Twyla laughs, sticking out her hand. "I'm Twyla."

"Twyla, these are my college friends, Ellery and Cooper."

They all shake hands.

"I gotta use your bathroom." Cooper steps into my apartment but turns around. "Sorry for being rude, but this is what happens when people don't let me use a public restroom because they feel the need to lecture me on germs." He stares at Elle, and she laughs.

"I was just saying." She shrugs.

"It was nice meeting you, Twyla." He waves and goes deeper into my apartment.

"She's engaged to Chase Andrews," I inform Elle.

Her eyes light up. "So you know Miles Cavanaugh then. They used to play together."

I elbow Elle to shut up.

Twyla glances at me and tilts her head. "Um… he's my brother. Have you not told your friends anything about your life back in San Francisco?"

Elle crosses her arms and stares me down. "What hasn't she told us?"

Twyla giggles. "She knows Miles. The two of them have this hate relationship that I'm not entirely sure…"

"Is hate?" Elle finishes, eyes sparkling.

Twyla points at her. "Exactly."

"Sounds like B," she says, nodding.

"Whatever." I roll my eyes.

"You can keep acting indifferent, but I heard it in your tone when you said you were moving here and how you were afraid it might look like you'd followed him."

"Which I did not. *Sportsverse* is a national publication and it's my dream. Even though I'm writing on the Tundra, and they're not even the national hockey team, it's a step into the magazine and that's all I need to prove myself."

Elle puts her hand on my arm and runs it up and down. "I'm just repeating what you said. We all know how important this job is to you."

"Definitely," Twyla says. She and Elle smile at each other then me.

"And it's probably a good thing that you're not writing on the Grizzlies because I'm not sure which one of you would kill the other first." Twyla hugs me. "Speaking of which, Miles is expecting me, and we all know how overprotective he is."

"He's probably on the phone with the police right now," I joke.

"Good luck, but you don't need it. You're going to do great here." Twyla squeezes me tightly. "Miss you."

"Miss you."

We step out of our hug, and Twyla wraps her arms around Elle, who isn't always so affectionate.

Elle stands with her hands at her sides at first then pats Twyla's back. "Bye, bye, now."

I bite my lip to keep from laughing because Elle looks so uncomfortable.

"Take good care of her," Twyla whispers loudly enough for me to overhear it.

Then she releases her, and Elle exhales a big breath.

"Love you, talk to you soon." Twyla waves before rounding the staircase and heading down.

"She seems nice. And friendly," Elle says.

"Too friendly for you, I know." I pick the pizza box back up, walk farther into my apartment, and she follows, closing the door.

"And she's Miles's sister. That's one piece of information you forgot to tell me."

I whip around, and the pizza box almost falls out of my hands. "Do not tell Coop anything. As far as he's concerned, I do not know Miles." She scrunches her eyebrows. "Oh Jesus, you already told him, didn't you?"

"No. I promise." She raises her hand. "But why not?"

"Because... I have my reasons."

"You don't want Coop to not like him? You're worried about Miles Cavanaugh and the team dynamic?"

I glance down the hall and see that the bathroom door is still shut.

"Cooper should make up his own mind about Miles," I whisper. "Promise me."

"Promise. I won't say anything, but he's eventually going to find out. You're going to be at some games with me this year. You know how lonely it was for me, waiting for him after the games when all those jersey-chasers were waiting to get a piece of him. I almost got into a fight every damn time."

I hadn't really thought about that, but still… I'll postpone Cooper knowing as long as I can. Maybe the distance between Miles and me will do us some good. We're not in the same social circle now, and I don't write about him. With time, maybe we can be cordial with one another.

"I'm starving." Cooper walks down the hall and opens the pizza box. "Fuck, Elle, I told you I wanted meat."

"And you also told me that camp starts next week and I shouldn't let you eat things your nutritionist wouldn't approve of. So if you're having pizza, you're having veggies."

He stares at the pizza as though someone told him he's eating liver for the next week straight.

"I was so excited," he whines.

"Stop being a baby," I say and grab three beers from my fridge. Grocery delivery is the best thing ever. I pop open the bottle and hand it to him. "Here, drink away your problems."

"She knows I don't like mushrooms," he whispers and takes his pizza and beer into the other room, where he turns on the television.

"It's just like old times now that you're back." Elle side-hugs me and holds up her beer.

I clink mine with hers.

"Welcome to Chicago, B."

Cooper runs over and clinks his bottle to mine. "Hey now,

you can't be leaving me out of your girly things now that we're back to being a throuple."

I raise my eyebrows. "We're not a throuple, Coop."

He stares at us for a second and busts out laughing. "I just meant we're three, not a... fucking hell, you know what I meant."

We laugh and he goes back into the living room, sits down, and eats his pizza.

As much as I'll miss my friends in San Francisco, I'm happy to be reunited with these two. I can't wait to see what excitement Chicago brings me.

My phone rings and I pull it out of my back pocket to see my mom's name. Elle looks over my shoulder and sighs. I hit Decline and she sighs harder.

"Sooner or later..."

"Not tonight," I say, grabbing my pizza and beer.

I was able to hide a lot of that part of my life in San Francisco, but here, Elle and Cooper will call me out on my shit. That's the problem with old friends. They know your wounds better than anyone.

CHAPTER 3

MILES

TRAINING CAMP...

Training camp isn't for the weak. It's the hardest training I've ever done. During my first training camp, I threw up ten times. I underestimated it. But now I know.

Thankfully, today is over, and I'm stretching while some of the players are working one-on-one with their specialist coaches. I'm sitting in the field, talking to my other defensive players, when Ronnie Michaels walks up to me.

Ronnie is the general manager of the Chicago Grizzlies. He's the one who positioned my trade last year. He's the one who brought me into his office my first day on the team and said how much they wanted me. How much of an asset I would be to the team. I felt great until the draft happened, and they took a safety in the fifth round. Why do the Grizzlies need a third-string safety?

He sits down beside me. Ronnie's one of those hands-on GMs, always telling you how he wouldn't be where he is without the players. Which is nice to hear, and of course, in a roundabout way, it's true. Without players, the league doesn't exist, but there'll never be a shortage of guys who want to play professional football.

"Great day today. That pick-six against Damon? Fuck, man, everyone went crazy."

I could say it's like flag football out there right now. We're not in pads yet and just running drills. The pick-six was nothing. But I'm going to take credit, because Cooper is one hell of a quarterback, and Damon Siska has some of the best hands in the league. So the fact I stopped them from scoring means I'm doing something right.

"Thanks. It was fun out there."

"And that's what it's all about. Fun. Too much serious shit in this league."

Says the man who doesn't have to fight for his position every year. The Grizzlies gave me a two-year contract. So in reality, I have to prove myself this year with the hopes they resign me.

"I can't tell you again how happy we are that we were able to get you onto the Grizzlies. You're going to do amazing things for us." He claps me on the back and stands. "I have to go tell the *Sportsverse* reporter just that. Come over when you're done, and I'll introduce you to her."

For a moment I freeze, not wanting to look in the direction he's headed for fear of finding a short, feisty brunette with a scowl. Because if Bryce was hired at *Sportsverse* to cover the Grizzlies, I'm going to lose my ever-loving mind.

Thankfully, when I look up, a tall redhead is smiling at me. Ronnie's already made his way over there, and he must say something about me because she waves and her smile grows. It would make my day if this woman were one of my fans and not the half of Chicago that thinks I'm a bust and past my prime.

After I finish stretching, I walk over to the press area where Ronnie is still talking to the redhead. With so much against me, I can't pass up an opportunity for good press.

"Hi," I say, and Ronnie turns to me, putting his hand on the back of my shoulder as if he's presenting me.

"Miles. So glad you could cut your stretching a little short and talk to us. Let me introduce you to Shelly Breckles. She's the point person for *Sportsverse Magazine*, and she covers the Grizzlies."

I put my hand between us and her thin, smooth hand slides into my calloused one. "Nice to meet you."

"The pleasure is all mine. I'm a Wolverine too, and I've been following you around ever since."

"Really? You went to the University of Michigan too? What year?"

"Just a year behind you."

"Really?" I can't believe I don't know her. I thought I knew everyone who wrote for the newspaper back then.

"Yeah, I had a talk radio show on campus where I'd go over the games. I was way too intimidated by you to ask you to be on it though. But here we are now."

"Exactly, here we are now," Ronnie says, clapping me on the back again. "I'm going to leave you two to catch up."

We say our goodbyes, and my eyes follow him as he makes his way over to the fifth-round draft pick, Tre Brummer. A sour taste hits my tongue. He's younger, faster, and was supposed to be drafted higher, except the idiot got into a bar fight, and now he's been labeled as a troublemaker.

"So..." Shelly pulls my attention back to her. "I was so excited when you were traded to Chicago. I went out and bought your jersey. I already have some interesting articles and pieces to do about you that I'm pitching to my editor."

"Why would you want to do that?" I shouldn't ask the question, but why would I be important enough to have special pieces on me?

Her green eyes widen. "Are you kidding me? You're like the underdog story of the year. You're traded mid-year and the team you were on for years wins the Big Game? Don't tell me you're not upset about that. That you don't feel like you have something to prove."

Shit, this woman understands me.

"Yeah, I do, but the Kingsmen deserved to win. Lee Burrows is one hell of a quarterback." Plus, he's my friend.

"So is Cooper Rice, and he's younger than Burrows. Analysts are saying this is his year, and with you on defense to stop the other teams, it's a match made to get you guys to the Big Game. That's all without even adding Damon Siska into the equation. You should be smiling, Miles." She playfully pushes my shoulder and laughs.

"There have been a lot of teams with great players that never reached the championship game."

She rocks back on her heels. "You're one of those, are you?"

I arch an eyebrow. "One of?"

"Pessimist."

I'm not sure that's what I would say. I shrug. But I know better than to get my hopes up. Maybe this year they'll want to trade me somewhere else just when we're on a winning streak.

"I learned a long time ago to keep my expectations low."

She laughs and hits me in the shoulder again. "Well, you have me on your side this year and I'm going to make sure everyone, including Ronnie and the whole coaching staff, know how good they have it with you as their first-string safety. Have faith in me, Miles Cavanaugh. You're going to be the hottest commodity in the league by the year's end."

"That would be amazing. I'm usually underrated." I smile at her.

"Exactly, but I could be president of your fan club. I love the way you play, the way you live your life away from the press, the way you take your physicality seriously with your workouts and watching what you put in your body."

My ego soars with her words. Finally, someone on my

side. Someone the complete opposite of Bryce and her nitpicky bullshit. "I can't tell you how happy you just made me."

She smiles wide. "I couldn't wait to get down here this morning. I tried on, like, five outfits. My boyfriend is jealous, but he's not really a sports guy, so he doesn't understand how I've followed you your entire career and how anxious I was to meet you in person. I felt like those young girls who cry at the concert of their favorite boy band." She laughs again.

I join in with her because I must be dreaming or lost in some other world because a sports reporter wants to scream from the rooftops how great of a player I am.

Fuck, maybe Chicago is exactly where I need to be.

———

Later that day, in the dorms where we stay during training camp, Damon and Cooper are playing some video game in the common area, so I sit in the chair next to them. I knew Damon Siska in college—we were teammates—so he made my adjustment to the Grizzlies a lot easier. Propped me up to the other players.

Cooper, on the other hand, I don't know much about, except that some woman on a social media app fell in love with his looks and made these videos that went viral, and women all over the world fell in love with him. He's been inundated with commercial deals and magazine covers over the past year. I've never been the "it" player, so I have to wonder how he handles all the fame, especially when it's not even football-related.

"Say thank you," Damon says, his thumbs moving on the controller, his eyes fixated at the screen.

"For?"

"I scored you a place at The Den."

Cooper laughs. "Shit, man, did you start that name for the place?"

Neither of them look at each other while they're talking, instead concentrating on the screen.

"Hell, no, man, but it's really brilliant when you think about it. I mean Grizzlies and The Den?" Damon laughs.

"Is someone going to fill me in about what The Den is?" I ask.

"It's our place on the North Side, by the Colts field."

The Colts are one of Chicago's baseball teams. The most-loved team on the North Side.

"People call where you live The Den?"

They glance at one another and laugh before concentrating back on the television.

"Tell me you get it, Cavanaugh?" Cooper says, his body twisting as though that can impact his game on the screen. "I know you're, like, a straight arrow and shit, but you do enjoy some of the advantages to being a pro football star, right?"

"Hell no, my bro doesn't," Damon says, his thumbs hammering on the buttons. "Fuck you, Rice."

Cooper smiles as he continues to win the video game.

"So how and why did you score me a place?" I ask.

"You're in that short-term rental still with shitty furniture and an even shittier location. You're not gonna meet any girls living where you are right now. So I pulled rank. After Creed retired, half the team put in bids for his floor."

Cooper glances in my direction and laughs. "It's a four-flat with a bar on the street level and a rooftop bar and bleachers that look onto the Colts' field. It's the top floor unit too. Premium. You really should thank him, because I heard some of the offers from other players were hard to pass up."

"Then why did I get the place when I never even expressed any interest in wanting to live there?" I ask.

"Because, like I told Burrows, you're under my wing here, and I'm not going to fail you like he did. Fucking bastard gets attached and lets you become a hermit?" Damon shakes his head like "how could he?" "We're going out, and you're going to enjoy your life for once. That means you live at The Den with Rice and me." He drops his controller and walks away, pulling at his blond hair. "Fuck this."

Cooper laughs. "It's just a game, man."

Having known Damon since college, I'm familiar with his hatred for losing at anything. Back then, he would've broken something.

"So, how much is this coveted spot in The Den going to cost me?" I ask.

Damon recovers quickly and laughs. "Rematch, bastard."

"It's worth the cost," Cooper says.

"So say thank you," Damon insists, picking up his controller, along with Cooper, to play again.

"Thanks, I guess, but I don't think I'm going to do the name justice." I'm not the playboy type, even if I wish I were.

"I'm gonna make sure you do. And you're welcome." Damon smiles at me before his lips turn into a thin line and he puts on his game face to compete with Cooper.

Things are looking up. I wanted to find common ground with my teammates, and with Shelly at *Sportsverse* on my side, maybe this is my year.

I fucking hope so.

CHAPTER 4

BRYCE

The nervous butterflies refuse to stop as I walk into the *Sportsverse Magazine* office building in downtown Chicago. Public transportation did not help my hair this morning because it was so hot, and I'm pretty sure all my makeup has dripped off my face.

I press the elevator button and ride it up to the twentieth floor. The doors slide open, and it feels as if people are tumbling in my stomach while I stare at the *Sportsverse* logo on the wall.

You've got this, Bryce.

You deserve this.

Do not fuck this up.

I step out and take a breath before turning to the right to see a large reception desk. Although I was already here for my final interview, I have no idea where to go, so I stop in front of the frazzled-looking woman.

She keeps pressing buttons on the phone and asking people to hold before clicking on another line. I hate to even bother her. A delivery guy who rode up the elevator with me stands next to me, staring at her. She blows a piece of her hair off her face and holds her finger up to us.

"She must be a temp," the delivery guy says to me. "She's not the normal receptionist."

I nod.

"What are you here for?" His gaze falls down my body and never makes it back up to my eyes.

Instead, it rests on my legs, and I reprimand myself for wearing this pencil skirt. If it wasn't my luckiest one, I would've worn something else. But I wore this when I got my job at the *Chronicle,* and I was wearing it when I got the call from *Sportsverse.* Good things happen when I wear this skirt.

"Today is my first day," I say.

His eyebrows lift.

I sigh. "Yes, funny thing, women in the world know a lot about sports too."

He holds up his free hand. "I didn't say anything."

"You didn't have to, your body language said it all." I used to be tighter lipped when men gave me the all-too-familiar look when they found out I'm a sports reporter, but I'm done with that.

"So you're a reporter then?"

I nod, waiting for the receptionist, but she's still fielding nonstop calls. "I am."

"For women's basketball or something?"

I spear him with a look. "Why would it be women's?"

He holds up his hand again. "I was just asking. I didn't mean to offend you."

"I'll be reporting on hockey."

"The Hawks?" he asks.

"Tundra."

"Oh." He says it in a tone that implies that this makes more sense to him.

I fucking wish I could've said the Hawks. There's a lot to report on with the Tundra. More shifting of players. Bringing them up, bringing them down. The ins and outs are fascinating, and I'm excited to report on them. But they aren't a national team, so it isn't considered as prestigious.

I turn back to the receptionist because I no longer want to talk to this man.

She finally stops and looks at me as if she's about a second from tears. Oh, I know that look.

I round the desk and pick up a second phone which must be used by a second receptionist who isn't here. Sometimes you just have to step in and take control of a situation.

"*Sportsverse Magazine*," I answer. "Please hold."

With the two of us double teaming the phones, me placing people on hold and her transferring them where they need to go, it's only a few minutes before there's a break in the calls, and everyone is taken care of.

"Thank you so much. Both receptionists called in and I'm a temp." She signs for the package and places it on the desk.

"Good luck, you two," the delivery guy says, and I roll my eyes.

"And what can I do for you?" she asks, turning her attention to me.

"Well, today is my first day. I'm to report to Bill Osterman."

Her eyes widen. "Oh, I'm so sorry." She shoos me away with her hand. "I'm holding you up. Mr. Osterman's assistant was adamant that I send you to the conference room as soon as you arrived. I guess it's a team meeting or something." She presses a button on the phone system. "I'll show you there."

"I'm sure I can find my way," I say.

"No. Better I do it. I already messed it up."

"Okay."

She leads me down the hall to a fishbowl of a conference room, which means I see them all before I enter.

It's filled with all the reporters I've read for years. Some I've looked up to for the majority of my career, and now I'm going to enter that room and be one of them. Sure, I'm not covering a national team—yet—but it's a stepping stone.

"Here you go. Knock 'em dead." She winks and rubs my arm as she walks away.

I inhale and exhale, place my hand on the door, and wrench it open, sliding through a sliver and trying not to be noticed, but Mr. Osterman is on me right away.

"Bryce!" he exclaims, as though I'm his daughter who just returned from college as a surprise.

I nod. "Hello, Mr. Osterman."

"Come on over." He waves me to the front of the long boardroom table where he sits.

I swallow, and it feels as though there's a walnut stuck in the back of my throat. Regardless, I walk over to him, putting on my best smile.

"Okay, gang, here's our newest reporter, Bryce Burns. She comes to us from the *San Jose Chronicle*, where the majority of her reporting was on the Kingsmen." He looks to me for confirmation and I nod. "I think you'll find she'll be a great asset to the team. She's known for her toughness, her no-holds-barred assessments of all players."

"Especially Miles Cavanaugh," a guy I don't recognize says. "What did you have against that guy?"

Mr. Osterman looks at me to answer. I don't report to that guy, and this is the kind of question you ask in a break room, not a boardroom.

I clear my throat. "I don't have anything against him. I'm not going to sugarcoat it when I see a player underperform-ing. If they have flaws, it's my job to report them just as much as I commend their talents."

Mr. Osterman nods, and the man looks pissed off. "That's exactly why she was hired. I'm done with the favoritism our prestigious magazine gets accused of year after year. Look at this morning, Grant. You reported on the Panthers training camp, and people are saying the GM wined and dined you so that you'd write that they're the team to beat this year. You know how many calls we've fielded this morning from other teams saying you're not playing by the rules?"

Holy shit, the guy who gave me a dirty look is Grant Thorn. He's the most well-known reporter here, and I did a whole report in college about his reporting style. The head-shot he uses must be at least fifteen years old because he looks way younger in his picture, so I didn't recognize him at first. He allowed a GM to lead him to write a story he might not really have believed. Despite that, he still seems to always land on his feet.

"I told you I want to talk to you about that privately." Grant looks at Mr. Osterman as though he's the one who holds the power around here. Then again, he might. I've heard about places where a reporter has more say than the top brass, and editors don't want to piss off their best and most popular reporters.

"And I said I was going to address it in the team meeting. Now, we're delayed enough. Everyone welcome Bryce." He turns to me. "Have a seat. Shelly was just about to give us her take on the Grizzlies this year."

I smile and slide into a chair at the back of the room. I know that Shelly Breckles reports on the Grizzlies because, in the end, it's her job that I want. I love all sports, but football is my favorite. One thing my dad did for me over the years was bred my love for the sport. But I'll get there eventually, I know it. And hopefully by then, Miles will no longer be playing for the team.

"I was at training camp last week, and it was exciting seeing Cooper Rice and Damon Siska work together. But watching Miles Cavanaugh on defense was what was really impressive." She looks at me. "Sure, he joined the team late last year, but I think the trade messed with his head because he didn't perform to his caliber."

That's putting it nicely. It's like he was lost out there

which, I'm sure she's right, had to do with the trade. Every week, the Kingsmen were getting closer to the Big Game, and he was letting people get past him. His head wasn't in it, and Shelly should have called him out for it, but I've read enough articles to know that she's a fan of his. Miles and I may not see eye to eye on much, but I want to see him succeed. It's not my job to prop up his ego though.

"I've always liked him. He's not flashy. Quiet demeanor. Shit, what other player gets his picture taken in public, reading on a park bench?" one of the men I don't recognize says, and the entire room laughs.

"He's definitely the opposite of his college teammate, Damon," another one adds.

"Which is why I feel like we should spin his story narrative this year," Shelly says. "My gut says this can be the Grizzlies' year, and if we cast him as the underdog, which readers will love, they'll be cheering him on all year."

"You're delusional if you honestly think the Grizzlies have a chance this year," Grant says. Everyone groans, and he raises his hands. "Regardless of what people say, I believe in the Panthers."

The room erupts in laughter.

"Didn't their star wide receiver just return from knee surgery? And their quarterback is a baby, drafted last year and not even first-round," an older woman says, and everyone nods. She makes good points.

Everyone takes turns talking about what they're covering until we're dismissed. As everyone files out of the room, Grant approaches me. My heart beats out of my chest as though I just swam across Lake Michigan.

"Just so you know, and I don't say this because what people are saying about me is the truth, people can't pay me off for my opinions, but you can't go into this like a guard dog protecting its bone. You're in the big leagues now, and you're lucky Miles Cavanaugh is as easygoing as he is because there are other players who will blacklist you. I suggest that you take this opportunity with the Tundra to learn the fine art of creative criticism. You have to boost the ego higher than you hurt it. Wait until you travel with a team, and you're with those players twenty-four seven who you like to be so 'honest' with." He puts the word "honest" in air quotes then sighs. "Good luck, but I don't really expect to see you around much after this season."

I stare at his back without saying a word, which is rare for me, but he literally stunned me silent. Though I can feel the rage creeping up my chest into my neck. My face will probably be bright red in a minute.

"Don't listen to him. He's a jerk," a woman says next to me.

I turn toward her. She has chestnut-brown hair cut to her chin in a sassy bob. Her wide-leg plaid pants paired with a blouse is a cute and sophisticated look. I'm pretty sure I own something similar. She looks a little younger than me, as if maybe she's just done with school.

She holds her hand out to me. "Rachel. I cover the suburbs baseball team."

"Nice to meet you. Bryce. Which you already know."

She smiles. "Don't worry about Grant. I interned here for two years through college, and he'd always give me advice, acting like he was my mentor. It was never good advice." We both laugh. "I've read some of your stuff."

"You have?" I blink in rapid succession.

She shrugs. "I applied for your position but didn't get it. I wanted to hate you, but I love your take. Just because they're professional athletes doesn't mean they're above criticism and always have to get their way."

"Do you want to go out for a drink tonight?" I ask, eager to be on friendly terms with at least one person at my new job.

"I'd love to."

I think this move will be good for me.

CHAPTER 5

MILES

can't believe the first game of the year is here. I moved into my new place at The Den, as they call it, and it's been good. I see Damon and Cooper quite a bit, and it's in a good neighborhood with lots to do.

Creed, who retired, left a lot of his furniture. Since I've been told he was a bigger player than Damon, I have a new bed coming. I should probably change out all the furniture, and in time, I probably will. Black leather isn't really my style. But I've stocked my fridge, unpacked my shit, and gotten settled.

Now I'm in the locker room, and the pep talk I gave myself earlier seems to be for naught, because my nerves are taking over.

The rest of the team seems so at ease. Damon isn't even fully dressed, walking around, razzing every player, while Cooper quietly puts on his gear. Eventually, the two of them start talking about the day they went to the rooftop of our building to watch the Colts baseball game. I was moving into the building that day and missed most of it. By the time I made it up there half the group was already gone.

Damon's having a fine time busting Cooper's balls.

Cooper's best friend Ellery, is a woman, and Damon thinks there's something more between them because Cooper doesn't want any of his teammates to date her, which I get. I felt that protective of someone who wasn't mine once upon a time.

"But I'd fix you up with B," Cooper says. "She loves sports, football is her favorite, and she's just a lot of fun to be around. Not much gets her in a bad mood."

I shrug. "I guess we'll see the next time you guys all hang out."

I'm still hung up on the fact that Bryce Burns lives in Chicago now. After my sister told me that my archnemesis moved here to write for *Sportsverse Magazine*, I was proud of Bryce because she wants to make a name for herself, but at the same time, I'd thought I'd escaped her. That I'd be able to start over without worrying about running into her. Maybe this Bea will help take Bryce off my mind.

"She and Elle are stopping in before the game. They used to do it in college, and I thought maybe it'd give us all good luck this season if they wished me luck before the game." Cooper shrugs. "I'm willing to do just about anything to win the championship this year."

Siska and I nod. We both want it too, like a burning need inside us. I want it to prove my worth, Siska because it pisses him off that Lee, our other college buddy, won it last year, and Cooper because I think he wants to prove he's more than just easy on the eyes.

We continue to get ready, and once we're all dressed, we sit around in a circle. Siska and Cooper are captains, so they lead the team with a talk that should get us hyped up to win. And they each do a great job.

I grab my helmet from the locker room as the door bursts open. Standing there in team gear is Elle with Cooper's number on her cheek and a shorter woman who has the Grizzlies mascot head on as she dances into the room.

This must be Bea. Even with a mascot head, it's easy to see that she has a sexy body. She's wearing Cooper's jersey, and her shorts show off her olive-toned legs with a pair of orange Converse. I'm already interested.

The team watches with laughter as they attack Cooper, giving him hugs.

"What the hell?" He lifts the mascot head, revealing a mass of dark hair.

When she laughs, my mouth hangs open and I realize that Bea isn't Bea, it's B, the first initial of the name Bryce. Her dark gaze lands on me, and there's no surprise in her eyes like there must be in mine.

She knew. Of course she did. My trade to this team wasn't a secret.

"Only you, B," Cooper says and brings her over to me. "B, this is Miles. Miles, this is B." Cooper's hand moves back and forth between us.

This is a telling moment. Will she reveal she knows me, or do we act like strangers?

"Hello, Miles," she says, lips pressed into a thin line and not hiding her displeasure.

Guess I have my answer.

I give her a curt nod. "Bryce."

"Do you two know each other?" Cooper asks, his head volleying between us.

"Of course they do. She's the one who wrote all that shit about Miles back in San Francisco," Damon interjects and laughs. "This is classic. How do you miss this stuff, Rice?" He walks over to his locker, thank God, to finish getting ready.

"Really?" Cooper frowns.

"Have you not read me?" Bryce sounds offended.

"I don't read anything about football. It'll fuck with my head."

Maybe I should be more like Cooper.

"Well, we just wanted to wish you luck." Ellery grabs

Bryce's arm, tugging her out of the locker room. "You guys have this. Go Grizzlies!" She raises her arm, with Bryce not bothering to look back at us.

She knew I'd be in this locker room. She's trying to fuck with me. Does she want me to do shitty out there tonight?

"Okay, time to fucking spill." Cooper sits down next to me.

"Fuck. Why were there two women in my locker room?" Coach Iverson yells, entering from the hallway. "Siska, I swear to God, if it has anything to do with you…"

Damon is quick to raise his hands. "No, sir. I would never."

The team snickers because we all wouldn't put it past him.

"Whoever it was, never again." He points at each of us, his face redder the madder he gets. "Now bring it in, because I have something to say."

We circle around, all of us dressed with our helmets in our hands.

"Rumor is that, to some, we're the team to beat. Rumor is that we're one of the teams who can get to the Bowl. Are you happy about that?"

"Hell yeah," one of the linemen says.

"Well get it out of your head! We're not playing for a fucking championship. We're not playing to be the best. Tonight, we're playing to beat one team. The fucking Stars. That's it. They've got fifty-two men, we've got fifty-two men. It's sixty minutes of hard work and sweat-producing effort. I've told every team I've coached from my son's peewee team to you now, you leave everything on that field. If you do, you'll get the results you want. So, Rice, count us down."

We all put our hands in, even though the guys on the outside of the circle can't really reach the middle.

"Three. Two. One. Grizzlies," we all say in unison.

Then some of us scream, others jump up and down, chest bumping some of the guys as we file out of the locker room, down the hallway, and spring onto the field as our fans scream and go wild. It isn't until I'm on our side of the field that I look up and see signs for Cooper and Damon, one or two for me and the other guys, but I'm not blind. I'm not their guy in Chicago. That title is being fought for between Cooper and Damon.

My gaze catches Bryce's. She's standing with Elle at the fifty-yard line, first row.

"I buy her season tickets every year," Cooper says, coming up beside me.

"Wonderful."

"So what happened between you and B? Whatever you're keeping secret, you should know that she's going to be at every home game as long as she lives here. You'll have to get used to it."

I look at him and he shrugs, walking away to toss the ball to his quarterback coach.

There goes the hope I had that I'd be starting over. My biggest critic will sit front and center at every home game and she works for the biggest sports magazine in the country. Perfect.

———

Every time we score, the Stars come back and score with us. I think we might have underestimated them, and they feel like they have something to prove because the game wasn't supposed to be tied in the fourth quarter with only three seconds left. The Stars are on the fifty-yard line with possession of the ball.

I squat down, ready for their center to hike the ball. As soon as I see the ball release, their wide receivers and running backs scatter.

"Go to the right!" I yell to Henderson. "Corner pocket. I'll cover the middle."

A wide receiver breezes by me toward the endzone, and I chase the fucker down. The crowd goes wild, but then all the noise disappears as I watch the ball spiral in the air. It wobbles right and then left. Fucking Chicago and their Windy City crap.

"You'll never get it, Cavanaugh," Evans, the Stars wide receiver, says to me.

But I stick to him, and both of our hands go up as soon as the ball falls from the sky. My left arm stretches, and I jump right in front of Evans, knocking the ball down, but my right hand grabs it before it hits the ground. I tuck the ball under my arm and run down the field. The crowd yells, and cheers explode around me, but I try to push it all away and concentrate on my job—to get this ball in the other end zone.

"Fucking hell, Cavanaugh. GO. GO. GO!" Damon screams from the sidelines.

Every one of our defense players tackles, and I do a spin move before diving into our end zone with the ball in my hands to score the winning touchdown.

The Jumbotron shows fireworks bursting, and my picture is put up there with all my stats just in case someone missed that it was me who deflected, caught, and ran the ball all the way downfield. It's the play of a lifetime, one I might never repeat, and damn, does it feel good as all my teammates stampede onto the field, picking me up and carrying me to the sidelines.

I see the hype. I've been the guy in the middle for years, never the guy on top.

I run on pure adrenaline as I fall off their shoulders, and Coach Iverson screams in my face that I'm fucking awesome.

I'm still pinching myself as reporters come to me for interviews. It's not that I've never been interviewed, but usually I'm the third or fourth person asked and that's if I had a great game. Defense is sometimes a thankless position, but today, it's what won us the game and I'm going to enjoy every second of the attention.

I'm so busy being chest bumped and clapped on the back that I don't realize until it's too late that Bryce is right in front of me.

"Congratulations, Miles. Great play."

"What, no critique on my form or my footwork? Don't want to complain about how I deflected and then caught the ball instead of just catching it right away?" I ask, like an asshole, and her lips straighten into a thin line.

"I was being polite. You know we're stuck in the same friends' circle here—again—so we need to be cordial." She crosses her arms, and her tight Grizzlies T-shirt shows a line of cleavage that makes my mouth salivate.

I hate that my body wants her.

"We're going out for drinks, and no one is saying no." Damon jumps and points at each of us.

"Guess I'll see you soon then," I say to Bryce after Damon moves on to another group, celebrating the win as though it was the championship.

"Seems so." She huffs, rolls her eyes, and turns around.

My gaze shouldn't be on her ass, but it is because I'd do just about anything to have my hands on her ass and pull her up so she's straddling me.

I shake my head. She made the decision a long time ago that she didn't want anything to do with me. I need to remember that any chance of us becoming more than enemies was sealed and vaulted away, never to be opened again.

CHAPTER 6

BRYCE

We're at Peeper's Alley, the bar on the ground level of Cooper, Miles, and Damon's building, waiting for the boys rather than at the stadium where we'd have to wait with all the jersey-chasers who want to hook up with them tonight. It's the diviest of all the bars on this end of town, but there's something comfortable about it. I like that it doesn't take itself too seriously.

"So, I want the tea on you and Miles. You're leaving something out." Elle sips her mixed drink and leans back in the booth.

We're in the back room of Peeper's to give the guys some privacy once they join us.

"There is no tea," I say before tipping my vodka soda.

"You act like I don't know you. I could read your body language in the locker room, and be careful because Coop can too. If he saw what I did, he's going to have something to say about it." Her fingers tap on the table.

She doesn't have long nails because she's an ER doctor, but she does get regular manicures with a pretty polish all the time. Elle always looks put together.

"Cooper was trying to set me up. I know him, and he singled Miles out because he thought I'd date him."

"He is your type," she says with a shrug.

I scowl at her. "No, he's not."

She chuckles. "Why would you say that?"

"Because I like loud guys. Ones I can banter with." She's delusional. I've never gone for a guy like Miles. At least not for anything that might last beyond a date or two.

"He's so smart you could banter with him for hours, and I know you, you probably love his sarcasm. Plus, he's gorgeous. Tall and muscular. Takes his career seriously."

"Can't take feedback. Has a chip on his shoulder and is way too serious about everything…" I negate her reasons with my own.

She laughs and shakes her head. "So, tell me… when did you sleep with him?"

I almost spit my drink on the table. "What are you talking about?"

"Now I know you slept with him, so give me the details."

I huff. Sometimes I can't stand that Elle knows me way too well.

"It only happened once," I murmur.

"Just once because of you or him?"

"Do you really want to know?" I finish my drink, and when Ruby, the owner of Peeper's Alley, walks past the door, I raise my hand. "Rubes, can you give me another one, please, and a shot of tequila?"

"Make it two, Rubes!" Elle shouts.

"The boys aren't even here yet. Slow down, girls." She shakes her head but heads to the bar littered with men drinking beer and talking about today's game.

"Now give me the details." Elle grins around her straw.

"So bossy, but fine. You cannot tell Cooper though." I stare hard at her, and she crosses her heart with her pointer finger then kisses the tip, moving her finger away from her lips. It's been our thing since college.

"It was two years ago. There was this gala for the Kingsmen," I say as my mind drifts back to that night...

Miles dressed in a tuxedo was something else. I tried to act indifferent, like it didn't affect me, but an ache formed between my thighs the minute I saw him. Drink in hand, talking with his teammates with that confident air I didn't know whether he faked or not. Truth be told, his intelligence was intimidating. When I looked up his background, I found out that he could have had an academic scholarship rather than his football one, and he made the Dean's list every year he was at the University of Michigan. He could also play any position on the field. Quarterback in high school, wide receiver then a safety in college. It was alluring the way coaches and analysts saw his potential in positions other than the one he had excelled at.

I stood in my cream-colored dress that highlighted my olive skin tone, and Shayna, my friend, cleared her throat.

"What?"

"Are you sure you hate him?" she asked, wrinkles in her perfectly arched brows.

I couldn't even remember when our hatred started. He came after me once about an article I wrote because he'd been playing like shit, and I defended myself to him. Somehow it all snowballed from there. He'd had a horrible season, and I was the newbie at the Chronicle, and I didn't want anyone thinking I'd gone gaga over the safety of the team I was covering. That's mistake 101 in journalism. You have to remain impartial. He was messing up, and I had to point it out or be called out myself.

He did turn things around the next season, something I praised him for, but he never mentioned the good things I said about him. Plus, he was known in the league as having a chip on his shoulder and never feeling like he got the credit he deserved. Sometimes I thought I was just an outlet for him to express that frustration.

I'd met Shayna, the team's new athletic trainer, at training camp and since she was new in town, we instantly became friends. I was her plus-one that night, and coming with her threw me into Miles's close-knit group. I was unsure how he was going to handle me being there. I'd prepared myself for a war of words that I was sure he'd win.

I was on the outskirts of the dance floor by the middle of the night, already prepared to tell Shayna I'd had enough and wanted to go home, when someone bumped into me, knocking my drink all over my dress.

"What the—?" I looked up into a pair of killer blue eyes. Eyes so clear they grabbed me and took hold. If only they weren't so filled with hatred.

"What are you doing standing right here?" he asked, and I balked.

"You're blaming me because you spilled a drink on me?" I plucked the wet fabric off my chest, and when I looked up, Miles's eyes were focused on the outline of my breasts, which were now visible.

"Well, you're standing in a high-traffic area."

In truth, I was lost in thought, thinking about my mom who'd recently gotten sick.

"You have a lot of nerve." I stomped around him and out of the ballroom, down a hall to the men's bathroom because the women's was lined up with waiting women.

"You can't go into the men's bathroom," he argued from behind me as we walked into the men's room.

"Watch me. I'm not going to wait politely in line while my dress dries and is ruined."

A man came out of a stall and stared at us for a beat.

"What?" I sniped.

He opened his mouth to say something, but Miles was quick to cut him off. "Get the fuck out of here."

The poor man scrambled, looking at the sink like he wanted to wash his hands, but he decided to just leave. Miles locked the door and turned around to face me.

"That's going to give you negative press. He probably thinks you're going to fuck me in here. I know how much you hate negative press."

Miles shook his head then grabbed paper towels from the dispenser. "He can think what he wants. People shouldn't believe everything they read." His eyes bore into mine with an expression that implied that everything I'd written was false.

"Haven't you done enough damage tonight? If you want to go after my writing, bring me some concrete examples of where I was wrong."

He patted at the spot on my dress, which was in the crevice of my breasts, and my heart rate picked up.

"I just don't understand why you have to be so hard on me." He looked up, and his hand didn't stop trying to clean up the red stain on my dress.

I swallowed hard. "I just..."

"What?" His voice was quiet.

"I..."

I'm not sure what happened, except something inside me said to kiss him. I rose on my tiptoes and placed my lips against his. The paper towels dropped between us onto the tiled floor, and his calloused hands grabbed my face, not allowing me to pull away.

Everything was frantic and rushed. As though we'd been hiding our attraction for years and had finally allowed ourselves to indulge.

I'm not sure I've wanted anyone like I did him in that moment.

There were late nights I'd wonder what Miles would be like in bed, and for some reason, I had this expectation of him being soft and loving, but whether or not it was just that moment or not, his mouth ravished me, his hands gripped me, commanding me to do his bidding. His lips trailed down my neck and I moaned, my fingers threading through his dark strands, urging him to keep exploring.

"Leave with me," he said. "Right now."

"Miles," I said with a plea because I didn't want the feeling to end. I didn't want him to take his hands off me.

"I want you so fucking bad, Bryce." He picked up my hand from behind his head and guided it down to his crotch, placing it on the hard length pushing against his tuxedo pants. *"You're the only one who can satisfy this."*

He stared at me, his thumb running along my cheek. I opened my mouth but didn't know what to say. We were different people. I knew it. He knew it. I should've kept it to messing around in the bathroom and not gone home with him, but the desperation in his eyes unleashed some part of me I kept locked away deep inside.

"You want me to beg?" he asked, slipping down my body until he was on his knees in front of me, his hands on my hips. *"I'll beg."* He rubbed his chin between my thighs, his hands collecting the fabric up my legs.

"Let's go," I said, unable to resist him.

He stood quickly, grabbed my hand, and we were out of the bathroom and into a cab before anyone could spot us.

My body buzzed with anticipation as his large hand slid up and down my leg, causing my dress to rise higher and higher, but never enough to give the driver a glimpse of my panties. Miles was playing me, and I fucking loved the teasing.

We drove to his condo, where he paid the driver and greeted the doorman before we stepped into the elevator. I waited for him to smash me against the wall, dig his thigh between my legs so I could grind on him as he kissed me breathless. But he barely touched me other than his thumb running the length of my pointer finger where our hands joined. It only made me want him more.

By the time he closed his condo door, and I stood in the large room with floor-to-ceiling windows, the San Francisco skyline shining bright behind me, I was the one who was ready to beg.

He came up behind me, and his fingers took hold of the zipper, slowly sliding it down my back while his breath floated past my ear. *"You're so fucking stunning."*

Shivers racked my body. I'd never had anyone like Miles. I moved to spin around, but his strong hands kept my hips in place. With his help, the dress fell to the floor, leaving me in only my panties and heels. I reached behind me, and my hand ran up and down his length while he kissed my shoulder and neck, his fingers hooking in either side of my thong and pulling it down.

I stood naked in front of him and heard him unbuckle his belt and the clink of the belt hitting his floor. His shirt was tossed to the couch in my peripheral, then his bare body was pressed to mine. He picked me up bride style and his lips devoured mine all the way to his bedroom.

I was dripping wet when he reached into the drawer and rolled a condom down his length. I went to roll over on my stomach, but he held me still, staring into my eyes as he entered me inch by inch until he was fully seated inside me.

We didn't take our time, and there wasn't a lot of foreplay. I think the anticipation did us in. He thrust inside me, and my arms wrapped around his neck as he continued to pound into me. I came for the first time without any clit involvement, and he stilled inside me, spilling inside the condom and collapsing on me. Then he kissed my shoulder and collarbone until he softened inside me.

"Stay," he demanded.

All I was thinking about was experiencing it all over again, so I nodded.

We slept together another two times that night until the dawn light shone through his windows. I grabbed my things and had my hand on the doorknob of his condo when Miles appeared behind me.

"Where are you going?" I could tell from his tone that we had different expectations for what the night had meant.

"Home. I completely forgot about Shayna. I left her last night."

"I'm sure Burrows got her home. Come back to bed. I make a killer breakfast."

If he meant the green smoothies he raved about, I wasn't interested.

Our eyes locked, and he must have seen something in mine. His head rocked back, and he nodded. "Oh, I get it."

"We hate each other," I reminded him.

"Do we?"

"You hate me, Miles. Last night was just sex. A reaction to wanting what you can't have."

He laughed, but it was hollow. I knew he wasn't a one-night stand kind of guy. "I'll call down and make sure whoever is on shift gets you a cab."

"Miles." Usually, I never cared if a guy felt there should be more than just sex, but guilt clung to me where Miles was concerned.

"See you around." He walked back to his bedroom and shut the door.

"And that was it?" Elle asks. "You broke the man."

I scoff. "I didn't break him. He's fine. It's been two years anyway."

"Have you talked with your mom?" Her question pisses me off.

"What does that have to do with what I just told you?"

She inhales and sips her drink, her nonverbal way of saying my past is fucking up my future. Typical Ellery. What's funny is that she can't see her best friend is in love with her, but whatever.

"Don't look now, but the boys just arrived."

I turn in my seat, and sure enough, Miles stands in the doorway, his eyes locked with mine. Damon clinks bottles with him as he passes by, and Miles's attention shifts to him.

As all the players join us in the back room, I feel the adrenaline of that night we shared still flowing through my veins. I've relived that night too many times to count over the years, but with Miles so near right now, it's the first time I've wondered what it would be like today if I'd played that morning differently. What if he was mine? What if I didn't allow my past to dictate my future?

I shake my head because Miles Cavanaugh hates me. And I hate him. We both know that. It's the one thing we can agree on.

CHAPTER 7

MILES

'm not usually a go-out-on-a-weekday guy because I treat my career like any other job. Regardless of practice times, I'm in bed early, early to rise, and a workout to start my day. But I should've figured when I agreed to move into the same building as Damon that I'd be going out during the week.

When he presented me with hockey tickets to the Tundra, I figured it'd be fun to go to a sporting event I'm not playing in. And I fell in love with hockey the first time Lee Burrows took me to his brother Kane's game. He's retired and coaching the Florida Fury now, but he was one helluva player. The way the hockey players are so agile on skates makes me look pathetic that I can't catch a football in the air before my opponent does.

I walk into the Tundra arena with Damon and Cooper.

"Where's Ellery?" I ask.

"She got called in, but she says she'll make it after shift change."

"Are you going to survive without her tonight?" Damon asks.

I shake my head. He's always razzing Cooper about his

feelings for Ellery. Damon doesn't understand why some things aren't his business.

"Fuck off," Cooper says as we arrive at our private box.

Although no one told me how we got the tickets, I have my suspicions that it has something to do with a certain brunette who started working for *Sportsverse Magazine*.

Sure enough, we enter and there she is, talking to some girl in the corner about something with a carrot between her fingers. The other girl has a short dark bob, and it swings as she nods profusely at whatever Bryce is talking about.

"B!" Cooper bellows and a few heads turn in our direction.

Some of their eyes widen, others act indifferent. If this is mostly *Sportsverse* employees, seeing a professional athlete out in the wild isn't anything they haven't seen before.

Bryce turns to us, and the mouth of the girl she's talking slowly opens and hangs there as she looks at each of us. We're big guys and take up a decent amount of space in a small box like this one.

"Hey, Coop." She eyes me. "I see you brought guests."

Damon laughs and slaps me in the stomach. "We're not guests. We're friends."

After Cooper releases her, Damon hugs her, bringing her up so her feet hang off the floor. Jealousy pricks at my skin like a needle.

"My friends know not to pick me up." She pats his back. Once her feet are planted back on the floor, she grants me her attention. "Miles."

I wouldn't call it a welcoming smile that crosses her lips, but it's a smile, nonetheless.

"Hey, Bryce. Thanks for the ticket," I say, playing nice.

"Sure. The more the merrier." She gestures to the woman she was talking to. "This is Rachel. She works for *Sportsverse*."

Damon is quick to approach with his hand out. "I'm the only available man out of these three. Damon—"

"Siska. I know." The girl giggles just like Damon likes them to.

Obviously Damon's pissing on his territory here if he's telling this woman both Cooper and myself are taken when that's not the case, not that I care.

"Last I checked, I was available," Cooper grumbles.

Bryce pats his arm. "It's so cute you actually believe that. Excuse me."

She walks away to mingle with anyone other than me, and Cooper looks at me with a perplexed expression. Does he really not understand why everyone thinks he's not available?

"Come on, let's go sit outside the box and see why some women love hockey players over us," I say.

Cooper groans. "I wish that were true in my case."

"Yeah, your life really sucks." I roll my eyes.

He laughs and we grab some waters before sitting in the seats provided with the box. The game is just beginning, and the Tundra take control of the puck.

"Man, they're fast," Cooper says.

They shoot, and the goalie blocks the puck from the net.

"Why do you think it's only one point per goal?" I ask. "Like, who decided how many points per score for each game? Why are we six for a touchdown? Basketball two per basket?"

"You'd think a hockey or soccer goal would be worth more than a touchdown. I mean, they're harder to get," Cooper says.

"Right? These games are tied a lot too."

We sip our waters, watching all the players skate around.

"Not to mention the endurance these guys have to have."

"Huh," Cooper says.

"What?"

"I don't know, I figured you'd spit out some reason. Like

the names of who invented what sport or some mathematical equation."

My forehead wrinkles. "Why?"

"Dean's list."

I shake my head because that's what everyone thinks. And I can't deny it—I am smart. I worked my ass off to be able to get an academic scholarship in case I was injured or hurt playing football.

"Sorry to disappoint you."

He props one ankle on the other. The crowd starts booing and I look up to see the red light lit up on top of the home team's net.

"Do better next time." Cooper laughs and boos along with the crowd.

It goes to commercial break and Ellery and Bryce come down to join us. Having no other choice, either Ellery sits by me and Bryce by Cooper or vice versa, since we're in the middle two seats of four.

"Elle," Cooper says, and she bends down to give him a hug. "How was your shift?"

"Exhausting. I need a massage." She sits down next to him, and Bryce looks as if she's about one second from bolting.

"Here, let my magic hands do some work," Cooper says.

Ellery turns her back to face Cooper, and he massages her shoulders while she moans about how good it feels. I raise my eyebrows, and Bryce bites her lip to keep from laughing.

"B, sit. I'm sure you've networked enough," Cooper says.

She hems and haws.

"I don't bite," I say, and her face turns red because we both know that I do. "Well…"

She slides by everyone and sits down, turning her body away from mine.

Before I can think better of it, I lean forward and whisper, "You're the only one here who knows I bite."

She sucks in a sharp breath and doesn't say anything. Doesn't look at me. Just pretends I never said a word.

As Ellery moans and tells Cooper how good it feels, I gulp down the rest of my water.

"Look!" Ellery points at the Jumbotron.

I don't want to look because I'm pretty sure we're on the screen, but if I ignore it, I'm the asshole football player who doesn't acknowledge the crowd. My gaze lifts to the screen and it's worse than just the camera operator recognizing us— it's Bryce and me on screen with a heart around us and Kiss Cam blinking underneath.

"Fucking hell," I murmur.

Bryce waves and shakes her head. "You'd think they'd be on you two over there. I mean, you're moaning like he's getting you off."

"Jeez, B." Ellery glares down the row at her friend.

"Sorry." Bryce continues to wave for the camera to move on.

The crowd boos and heads in the arena turn in our direction.

"Just kiss me. It doesn't have to be a big deal," I mumble.

She flips her head in my direction, eyes scathing. "I'm not going to kiss you on national television."

"This isn't a national team."

She huffs. "Is that some kind of dig?"

"I just meant, hardly anyone is going to see it, if it's that you're ashamed to kiss me."

She faces me, her small hands balled into fists. "Why would you say that? Because I didn't fall on my knees begging for a relationship after you fucked me?"

"Whoa, what?" Cooper turns his attention to us.

"Coop, you were just getting the knot out," Ellery whines and cracks her neck.

"Did you not hear what I just did? When did the two of you have sex?" he asks.

I shake my head. Thank God Damon wasn't down here to hear it. I'd never hear the end of it from him. "Why are you bringing it up when you're the one who wanted to forget it even happened?"

I am not going to tell her I'd thought maybe it could've been the start of something. Hell, I'd never had chemistry like that with anyone. Her reaction to my hands on her was addicting.

"Just forget it." She leans forward to address Cooper. "Pretend you didn't hear that. And don't tell anyone."

"But I did," Cooper says innocently, and I almost laugh, until something catches the corner of my eye.

The abominable snowman mascot runs down the short stairs and stops beside Bryce. She looks at him and her cheeks turn pink. He has roses in his hand and everyone around us is staring because we're *still* on the big screen.

"Fuck, man. They don't mess around," Damon says from above us where he's standing in the suite.

He's right.

The character they call Tundra hands me the roses, and my eyebrows go up to my hairline. I forgot that they do these things to make the outing fun for the fans. I'm not usually a spectator. Who knows how long Tundra is going to be up here bothering us?

I accept the roses, and the mascot signals for me to give them to Bryce.

"Don't give them to me," she says so low I'm the only one who hears her.

"Just put on an act and smile," I mumble back.

"This is ridiculous." She huffs again. "I should never have sat here."

Tundra takes my wrist and forces me to move the flowers in front of Bryce then guides my wrist back to my lap, signaling that that's what I'm supposed to do. As if I don't know how to hand a woman flowers. If it were any other woman, she'd already be holding them, but Bryce always has to make everything more difficult than it needs to be.

I move my arm over in front of her and drop the flowers in her lap.

The mascot turns to the crowd with his thumbs down, and everyone boos. I'm in fucking hell, and I can hear my buddies cracking up beside me. Pretty sure Cooper wouldn't like it if he were the one on the spot and having to do all this for Ellery.

Tundra picks up the flowers and gives them to me again. This time I hold them out to Bryce, and she yanks them out of my hands.

When Tundra turns to the crowd again, everyone boos. He puts up his two pointer fingers and brings them together telling us we should kiss.

"Give it a break, buddy," Bryce says. "I'd hate to write a story about the Tundra mascot for *Sportsverse*."

"You give me a break, lady. I'm just trying to make the fans happy. You think I want to wear this ridiculous thing?" Tundra says so only we hear him. "Why won't you kiss a professional football player?"

"Because I shouldn't be forced to kiss anyone." Bryce crosses her legs and arms.

"You're a real buzzkill," he says and turns around to the crowd, holding his hands up in the air as though he can only do so much.

Everyone is pointing their thumbs down and shouting at us now. Jesus.

"They take the Kiss Cam pretty seriously here," Cooper says. "You're gonna be all over the news tomorrow as the people who can't play along."

He's right, and Bryce might not thank me for this now, but she will in the future.

I slide my hand to the back of Bryce's head and pull her toward me. My lips land on hers and she stiffens, her one hand landing on my chest, pushing me back. Then she relaxes into my hold just like that night in San Francisco. She shakes for a moment as if all the tension is leaving her body before she sinks into our kiss. I don't attempt to use tongue because I don't want her to punch me in the balls. Satisfied, the crowd goes crazy, screaming and cheering.

She ruins it when she pinches my nipple.

I release her, grabbing my aching chest. "Fuck."

We both stare at the screen and there we are, kissing. I hate to admit it to myself, but we look good together even though we'll never be a couple.

"I can't believe you." She stands once the game starts and the fans' attention is drawn back to the ice.

"They weren't going to stop until we kissed. Problem solved."

"And now my boss is going to think I just go around kissing athletes."

I stand and step in front of her. "Keep acting indifferent to me, Bryce."

Her chest rises and falls, but she says nothing. We both know what we felt in that kiss. She can deny it all she wants, but our desire for each other is still living under the surface of our hatred, and I'm pretty sure it'll stay there until the top blows off again.

CHAPTER 8

MILES

'm waiting at an outside table for two at a café downtown Chicago. Shelly Breckles from *Sportsverse* called me to meet to talk about the article she wants to write on me. She hasn't started traveling with the team yet because last weekend she was ill, which was when we were originally supposed to talk about it.

My phone vibrates, and I pull it out of my pocket and see my sister's name on the screen.

"If Chase is within five feet of you, I'm hanging up," I answer.

I'm just picking on her, but I don't understand why Chase always has to be touching her. I mean, c'mon—have some respect for the older brother.

"I cannot believe I'm finding out that you and Bryce are a couple from the internet! Why did neither one of you tell me?"

I groan. "What are you talking about?"

My phone vibrates in my hand.

"Check out the picture I just sent you."

I pull the phone away from my ear and open the text

message from Twyla to find an image of Bryce and me kissing at last night's Tundra's game.

"Oh, that."

"I'm sorry? Oh, that? What does that mean?" She's practically shrieking in my ear.

"You sound upset," I say, mouthing "thank you" to the server who sets my iced tea in front of me. "Does it bother you that I might be dating your friend?" I don't know why I bother leading her down a trail that's going to finish in a dead end. Maybe I'm curious what she has to say on the subject since she's in a relationship with one of my best friends.

She squeals, and I have to pull the phone away from my ear for a beat. "So you *are* dating?"

"No way," I deadpan.

"Miles!"

"Jesus, sunshine, it's early," Chase says in the background.

"Sorry, look at this." I hear kissing noises because she has me on speakerphone. "They're kissing but not dating," Twyla tells him.

Chase grunts, and I laugh because he doesn't give a shit about my life as long as I stay out of his with my sister.

"Don't get so worked up, it's not good for the baby," I say to distract them.

"You got my hopes up," Twyla whines.

"Why would you want me to be with Bryce? We obviously hate each other." I sip my iced tea.

"You only *think* you hate each other. This kiss proves it!" If she was here, she'd probably be poking me in the chest.

"Your hormones are making you see things that aren't there. We were forced to kiss for a Kiss Cam, that's all." It's easier to convince people I don't want anything to do with Bryce when, in reality, I would've loved to take her home last night. It took every ounce of my willpower not to slide my tongue between her lips. But admitting that to my sister will only give her false hope for something that's never going to happen.

"Keep telling yourself that. You're going to have a lonely life, big brother."

I spot Shelly climbing out of a car at the corner, and I lift my arm in greeting. She smiles.

"I gotta go. Keep that baby safe, and give Chase a good knee in the balls for me. Love you."

"Miles—" she pleads, but I hang up and pocket my phone.

Shelly winds through the iron gating for the temporary patio that's put up for the warmer months in Chicago, of which there aren't a ton. I'm already dreading the winter. Talk about a welcome—the day I was traded, there was a winter storm with winds so strong my face was numb by the time I walked across the sidewalk from my Uber to my condo building.

"Miles, good to see you." She holds out her hand.

I stand and shake it before pulling out the chair for her. She sits down and puts her hand over her stomach.

"Sorry, whatever this is, it's taking over my body." She laughs.

"How are you feeling?" I ask.

"Better now, but not a hundred percent. Sorry I missed the Minneapolis game, but you were a monster out there. I must say, I'm your biggest fan, but you're really making a name for yourself this season."

"Thanks. It's weird, I think I'm possibly playing the best I have in my career."

She frowns. "Certainly better than how you started out last year here. That was to be expected—new team, new dynamic, new plays. It all goes together, and of course you'd be nervous. And then for the Kingsmen to win..." She shakes her head. "That's the thing about sports, you can't predict the future. There're so many variables."

I nod. "Truth."

The server comes over, and Shelly orders a coffee. "Sorry, lately I just can't stay awake." She widens her eyes. "Okay, so…" She bends and digs into her bag. "I was talking to my editor, and he's on board with the highlight piece. I wanted to go over what that means and a few other things."

"Okay."

Her coffee arrives, and Shelly looks at the server as though she just threw Shelly a life vest in the middle of the ocean. "Thank you." She leans forward. "Could I bother you for a muffin too?" She looks at me. "Sorry. Rough morning."

"No problem."

"Don't worry, it's not contagious." She sips her coffee, moaning as she swallows. "Okay, let's get this going."

She pulls out an edition of *Sportsverse* with my friend and quarterback for the San Francisco Kingsmen, Lee Burrows, on the front. It was from last year.

"I know you recognize this guy." She flips through the pages. "As you know, it was a big deal for Lee to get this cover last year. Everyone thought it was his year, and then when he married during the off-season… everyone was dying to do a piece on him."

I nod, remembering Lee complaining about all the heightened interest in his personal life.

She opens the pages filled with pictures of Lee at all different ages with different football jerseys on and throwing the ball. Some pictures are of him with his brother, talking about how they're both involved in professional sports. Then there are some of his and Shayna's place. Her on the field with him, taping his ankle, and a few more of the two of them at home.

I hope this isn't the angle she wants to pursue with me because I don't have any of that. All I have is the sport.

While I'm flipping through the pages, Shelly asks, "I don't want to pry, but are you dating Bryce Burns?"

I inhale a deep breath. That kiss for the Kiss Cam was a

huge mistake. Maybe Bryce was right, though I'd never admit that to her. "No. The mascot wouldn't take no for an answer, so we just kissed to get the attention off us."

She stares at me for an uncomfortable minute. "When I talked to Bryce this morning, she said *you* kissed *her*."

"Yeah, but only to get the mascot to go away."

She nods. "Okay, I just wanted to make sure, because if we did a piece on you it would look like favoritism if you were dating one of our own. You can see that, right?"

I hold up both hands in front of me. "I promise you, I'm not dating Bryce Burns."

She smiles wide. "Great. So your article would be a little different than Lee's. His was about how his life was evolving. Marriage and kids change a player's perspective, as you've probably witnessed in the locker room."

I swallow down past the Sahara Desert level dryness in my throat. I know I have time, but I wouldn't mind having someone to share my life with. If I continue hanging out with Damon, I'm just going to end up with a bunch of booty calls.

"Yours would center more on your career journey. The different positions you played. Concentrate heavily on you being offered both athletic and academic scholarships out of high school. It changes things when an athlete graduates college on the Dean's list with the GPA you did, all while playing football. I'm going to be honest with you though, a lot of discussion will be about the trade last year and the Kingsmen winning after your departure. My editor wants to paint you as the underdog, and so do I."

Underdog? I feel like I've been that guy my entire life.

"Okay, but it's not going to be a pity piece, right?"

"Of course not." Without warning, she grimaces and hunches over, gripping her stomach. "Oh my god."

"Are you okay?" I start to stand, but she raises her hand.

"I'm fine. It's okay."

"Okay." I sit back down, but her face has lost all color.

The server comes over with her muffin and stops at the edge of the table. "Are you guys okay?"

"I'm fine. It's her." I point at Shelly, who's clearly still in distress.

"I probably just need to eat." She takes the plate from the server and tears the top off the muffin like a ravenous animal. She swallows it all in one bite and downs it with a heavy gulp of coffee. "That should make me feel better."

I stare at her because I'm worried something is really wrong. Maybe it's her appendix or something.

"Not a pity piece. Just an article to showcase you, show you off, let people know who you are and what makes you tick. We want them to know you're here to win and plan to do exactly that with the Grizzlies." She looks a little more comfortable now, so I relax back into my seat a bit.

"That all sounds great. I'm in."

"I hoped you'd say that. Let me grab my notepad and we can chat about what an article might look like." She bends down to her bag again and screams, falling off the chair and onto all fours on the concrete.

I bolt up out of my chair and hunch down beside her, unsure what to do.

"Something is wrong. It hurts so bad." Her hand covers her stomach.

"Miss, are you okay?" A woman comes over from a nearby table, and Shelly nods that she's okay, but I shake my head to indicate that no, she's not okay. "I'm a physician. Where does it hurt?"

Shelly goes over her pain and the flu symptoms she's had lately while the woman helps her back into her chair.

"Have you gained weight recently?" the woman asks.

I look at the server with an expression that says no one is ever supposed to ask a woman a question like that.

"A little, but I moved in with my boyfriend, and he's a pastry chef, and he makes treats all the time. What does that have to do with this?"

The woman glances at me and I think I know where she's going with this. *Holy shit.*

"Is there any chance you could be pregnant?" she asks Shelly.

Shelly opens her mouth. "I don't… no way. I mean… hold on." She pulls out her phone and scrolls through it for a moment, biting her lip harder and harder the more her thumb moves across the screen. "Shit, my period is never regular, but I haven't had it in months."

"Like a lot of months?" the server asks.

Shelly nods, fear in her eyes, clutching at her stomach again.

"I better tell my manager." The server rushes off.

The doctor's phone rings, and she pulls it out, her lips turning down. "I'm being paged to head back to the hospital for one of my patients." She looks at me. "Get your girlfriend to the hospital right now. Like, get into a cab and tell them to drive fast. You should have enough time." She holds up the edge of Shelly's dress and waits for permission if she can look underneath. Shelly nods, and I turn around so I'm not looking. "Yeah, you need to get there now."

"Is, like, the head out?" I ask.

"No, but it might be soon. Get going."

We thank her, and she stands and grabs her things from the nearby table, kissing the man she's with on the cheek before heading down the sidewalk.

My eyes widen. "We need to call your boyfriend."

"He's on a plane headed to some convention. Oh my god, I can't be having a baby! How did I not know I was pregnant? Who doesn't know they're pregnant!" she shouts. She's looking at her stomach that isn't anywhere near as big as you'd expect it to be.

She grabs her phone to hand it to me. I'm not sure who she wants me to call, but during the exchange, she accidentally drops it in the water glass. I grab it out right away but it's dripping with water and the screen is black.

Why does she have such an old phone? They're all waterproof now, aren't they?

I press the button on the side, but nothing happens. "Who do I call? Do you know their number?"

She screams, and the server returns with the manager.

"We have to go." I rush over and help Shelly up and over to the curb where the manager has hailed us a cab.

I have no idea what to do or who to call, so once we're in the back of the cab and it's moving, I grab my phone to call the only person who might be able to help her.

Surprisingly, she answers on the first ring.

"God damn you, Cavanaugh, do you know how many people are asking me about that damn kiss?"

Shelly screams beside me, clutching her stomach in pain.

"Who is that? What the hell is going on?"

"It's Shelly from your office. She's having a baby."

"A baby? She's not even pregnant, you idiot."

"Well, I'm pretty sure she is pregnant because a baby is coming out of her."

Bryce is quiet for a beat. "And you called me, why?"

"I don't know what to do."

"And I do?"

"Just… I don't know." I look over at Shelly. "Breathe… one… two… three."

She follows my instructions, taking deep breaths.

"Just help me?"

"How convenient that now you want my help."

"Bryce!"

"Fine. What hospital? I'll see what I can do."

I ask the driver, and he tells me where we're headed.

"Cook Memorial," I tell Bryce.

"Fine. I'll see you there."

She hangs up, and I continue to help Shelly breathe through pain that looks as excruciating to me as when I've seen guys tear their ACL. I've never been so happy to be a man.

CHAPTER 9

BRYCE

arrive at Cook Memorial and follow the signs to the labor and delivery department.

After a lengthy explanation as to who I am and why I'm here to see Shelly, I'm finally given a visitor's pass and told which room she's in. I try to keep my head forward, but some of the screams cause me to take a glimpse into some of the rooms. All I see are exhausted women, some begging for drugs, others swearing at their loved ones. A rare few lie there looking content, and I assume that's because they've already gotten their drugs.

Shelly's room is the farthest down the hall, and I knock softly in case she's already given birth, which I'm praying has happened. When I poke my head in, Miles is in a chair, looking as stressed out as I've ever seen him.

He bolts up as soon as he sees me. "I'll be right back," he says to Shelly, who I can't see from where I'm standing.

"Well hello, Daddy." I laugh, but he takes me by the elbow and guides me over to the window on the other side of the hall that has a small bench in front of it.

He spins me around. "You have to take over."

"Um… no. I'm only here because no one knows who Shelly's boyfriend is, and he's not listed in her paperwork, her parents are. And human resources doesn't want to call them because they have privacy concerns about the situation. They didn't even know she was pregnant."

"Supposedly, she didn't either," Miles says, raising his eyebrows.

You hear stories and there's a television show about it, but I'm still baffled by the concept. Then again, she didn't look pregnant. Maybe if you're going through your life, and it's hectic… who knows?

"I don't even know her," I say softly in case she can hear us.

"I don't either." He runs his hand through his hair. For a moment, I'm distracted by his long fingers and remembering them inside me. His blue eyes watched mine for a reaction to what he was doing. "Bryce!"

I throw up my hands and pretend I'm paying attention. "I'm not sure what you want me to do. I've never had a baby or helped deliver one."

"Well, her phone is ruined. I mean, who has such an old phone that it can't get a bit of water on it without crapping out?"

"Those of us who don't make millions, Miles, those who make things last as long as they can."

His eyes narrow. "Don't make me sound like a pompous ass."

"You're doing that all on your own. I'm just telling you how us common folk think."

His face twists. "You have no idea what you're talking about."

"Excuse me." A nurse approaches, and we turn to see her standing in the doorway of Shelly's room. "She's almost ten centimeters dilated, and things are moving fast now. The doctor is on his way to deliver the baby."

"Great. So, one of you will stay with her, right?" Miles looks between the two of us.

The nurse looks to me for clarification that Miles is in fact an asshole.

"Oh, he's not the dad," I say.

"We know. She's been very open about the fact that he's Miles Cavanaugh who plays for the Grizzlies." She shrugs as if she doesn't know the meaning of that.

I take in the pissed-off expression on Mile's face. In his world, he probably thinks everyone should know who he is.

"I'm just her coworker and I barely know her," I say. "We can't get a hold of her boyfriend."

A scream sounds from Shelly's room, and all three of us look in that direction.

"Well, the baby is coming," the nurse says. "Of course, the doctor and I will be in there, but it would be nice for her to have someone else there."

"I'm sure she doesn't want a man in there," Miles says, stepping back as if it's as easy as that.

"Miles!" Shelly screams.

I crack up before biting down on my lip to stop myself. He narrows his eyes at me.

"Listen, you two, having a baby is hard work, and she needs a village. For some reason, you two are here. You might not be her best friends in the world, but you're not strangers either. I've witnessed too many women come in here and go through a life-changing experience with no one by their side. Sure, we'll get them through the delivery, but it's not the same. And being that she's had no prenatal care, we don't know what to expect. So, I'm suggesting that it would be nice if you two both let her know she's not alone in this."

Miles turns to face me, and I sigh in resignation. All three of us walk into the room, because clearly neither of us would tap out on someone in need. It's one side of Miles I've always respected—the way he's always been there for his sister and his teammates. Selfish would never be a word someone would use to describe Miles.

Seconds after we've entered the room, a doctor joins us, clapping once. "Are we ready for this?"

He smiles wide, and I can't lie, the man is attractive. Sandy-blond hair just peeks out of his scrub cap with a tall, lean body and his green eyes sparkle with kindness.

The nurse motions to the two of us. "Dr. Turner, this is—"

"Miles Cavanaugh!" His eyes go wide. "I know you've been with the team for a bit now, but welcome to the Grizzlies. That pick-six from two weeks ago, holy shit, insane." He shakes his head as if he can't believe it.

Miles actually looks embarrassed, his cheeks turning a soft shade of pink. It's endearing. "Thank you, but what I do isn't nearly as important as what you do."

"Hello! I'm having a baby!" Shelly shouts, and our small huddle scrambles over to the bed.

The doctor washes his hands and puts on gloves then introduces himself to Shelly.

"Hello, Doctor McDreamy," she says.

"Dr. Turner gets that a lot." The nurse smiles. "Okay, if the two of you want to get on either side of her."

The doctor sits on his stool at the end of the bed and looks under the sheet as her legs are in the stirrups. I'm not sure I would want him between my legs as I'm having a baby, and I sure as shit wouldn't want Miles to see me in this state. Shelly's face is blotchy, she's sweating, her robe is disheveled, and she's one push away from her tit falling out right in front of him.

"Thank you both for being here. I have no idea what my boyfriend's number is, although he's on a plane anyway. He got a new phone a bit ago, and I just programmed it into my phone. I just hit his name when I want to call him." She has tears in her eyes, her head volleying back and forth between us. Then her smile dims and she squeezes my hand, harder and harder until I'm looking at Miles with my mouth hanging open because holy shit, it hurts. "Tell me I can push."

Dr. Turner peeks his head out. "You can push, Shelly. Let's meet your baby."

She leans up in bed, and I instinctively move my hand to her back to help her stay there. Her face turns as red as ketchup, and her grip on my hand gets even tighter.

"Just so we're aware, I need my hands to play," Miles says, cool and calm across from me.

I glare at him. "She's pushing a human out of her vagina."

"I'm just saying, they are my career, my money-makers."

Shelly falls back down on the bed, sucking in a deep breath.

"We're going to go again to ten. Just a few deep breaths. When I say go, you push, okay, Shelly?" the nurse says in a soothing voice.

We each try to extricate our hands from Shelly's, but she doesn't allow it.

"I think what Shelly's going through is a little harder than your hands hurting," I say.

Miles balks, his eyes finding mine and locking. "I'm sure if I broke all your fingers, you'd be complaining. That's how you make money, writing judgmental articles about athletes."

"Oh my god, of course you bring that up. It's my job to critique. No one wants to read an article that says this player does everything right. And hello, there is no player who does." My volume escalates.

"You two, you need to calm down and make this a calm place for Shelly," the nurse says.

But I can already see the fire in Miles's eyes. "Do you have any idea how hard it is to go out there and perform? Have all your mistakes and flaws out there in front of the world to see? After a shitty game, you have to read and hear people nitpick every single thing you did. Every bad thing you already think about yourself is right there for public consumption."

"No one made you become a professional athlete. It's not as if you're not compensated for the downside."

"Are you suggesting I get paid too much for what I do?"

"Push," the nurse says.

Shelly grips our hands and leans forward again. The nurse counts her down, then Shelly falls back against the mattress with a huge exhale of breath.

"All professional athletes get paid too much. Look at Dr. Turner. He's bringing new life into the world and doesn't come close to making what you do. You catch a ball for your millions—or in your case, you don't."

As soon as the words are out of my mouth, I regret them. I went too far and let my temper get the best of me. Normally I would apologize, but I'm so fired up, I'm not willing to give him the satisfaction.

"You're not even good enough to write about our team— or any national team, for that matter."

I huff. "It's called earning your stripes."

"Enough, you two," Shelly says. "I trump both of you right now. Woman in labor!"

"Sorry," Miles says with a frown.

"Yeah, I'm sorry." Why do I let this man drive me so insane?

After a few more rounds of pushing, Dr. Turner announces the birth of Shelly's baby boy. He comes out screaming, covered in goo, with a little cone head.

"Does anyone want to cut the umbilical cord?" He looks at Miles, clearly not understanding that neither of us are related to the baby.

"Pass," Miles says, and I can't help but laugh. This entire situation is ridiculous.

Miles looks at me, and we share a soft smile with each other.

Shelly lies on the bed, looking exhausted.

They do a bunch of checks on the baby and, after a few minutes, declare him healthy, and the nurse brings the baby over and rests him in Shelly's arms. In all the chaos and arguing with Miles, I lost sight of the fact that this little miracle was about to be born. In retrospect, it was beautiful to be part of.

"Thanks for allowing us to share this with you," I say, brushing my finger over his tiny ones.

"Thank you both. I can't believe I have a baby," she says and kisses his forehead.

I can't imagine how Shelly must be feeling, but it's clear that she's not upset about the fact that she's now a mother.

"Now you have to think of a name," I say.

She nods, but she's clearly enamored with her little bundle of joy.

Twenty minutes later, Miles has held the baby, and I'd be the world's biggest liar if I didn't admit that my ovaries were about ready to burst at the sight. Hot, muscled, giant football player holding a newborn—it's almost as big a turn-on as porn.

The nurse comes over. "I'm going to take him for a few tests just as an extra precaution, and you get to rest a little bit."

"Is he okay?" Shelly holds the baby a little tighter to her chest.

The nurse gives her a reassuring smile. "Everything seems to be perfect. We just need to be extra cautious since there was no prenatal care." She picks up the baby, and Shelly yawns.

"We'll get out of your hair too," I say. "Congratulations."

"Thanks."

Miles brings over the phone that's currently broken and places it on the table next to her. "In case it works."

"Thanks. I'll call my parents in a bit. They've had the same number for decades."

We all share a laugh then say our goodbyes, and Miles and I leave the hospital room.

"I feel like I should spend the night or something," I say. It's my worst fear that I'd give birth without the father of my baby present. That I'll pick someone like my father. I don't know why I was so resistant to helping her when I first arrived.

"I know. I can't imagine not knowing my baby was born because I'm on a plane and my girlfriend doesn't know my number by heart."

We step into the elevator together, and surprisingly, no one else is on it.

"I'm sorry for what I said." My nasty comments from earlier have been weighing on me ever since.

"Me too," he says.

When the elevator doors open and we're on the main floor, we walk out onto the Chicago sidewalk, where we're greeted with a wall of humidity. We stand there awkwardly for a moment, neither of us really knowing what comes next. We just shared a bit of a surreal experience that neither of us was expecting.

"Would you want to go grab something to eat?" he asks.

I'm unsure how to answer. But I don't get the chance.

"B!"

I turn and Ellery is walking toward me with some guy in blue scrubs, to-go boxes of food in their hands.

"I'll let you two talk. See you later," Miles says and walks away before I can say anything.

As I wait for Elle to reach me, a text comes through on my phone and I pull it out of my purse.

Mr. O: Shelly's officially on maternity leave, and since you have experience covering a national football team you'll be taking over the Grizzlies from here on out. I'll move Rachel over to cover the Tundra for the time being. Let's chat tomorrow.

My gaze lifts to watch Miles's back as he walks away, and I blow out a breath. Why are things so complicated between us?

I already know the answer—me.

CHAPTER 10

MILES

After Friday's practice, we all shower and make our way to the big room that fits the entire team, per Coach's instructions. It's more like an auditorium, so everyone can see the whiteboard with the coaches' notes.

"What could this be about?" Cooper asks. "I was gonna meet Elle for lunch and then help her pick out a new couch."

"You gonna break in the new couch too?" Damon laughs at his own joke.

"Your dick is gonna get you in trouble. All you think about is sex." Cooper points between Damon's legs and opens the door.

Half the team hasn't shown up yet, but it wouldn't matter if the room was jam-packed, I'd still notice the woman standing up front talking to Coach Iverson and Ronnie Michaels—Bryce. She's dressed in lavender pants and a sleeveless cream-colored blouse. Her heels make her appear taller than normal although she's still petite.

"What is she doing here?" I ask Cooper.

"Who?" Cooper follows my line of vision. "B!"

She looks up, smiles and waves to Cooper. But when her gaze shifts in my direction, she turns away. It doesn't make me feel any better about the ending of our last interaction. I could tell she didn't want to grab something to eat with me. She was probably happy Ellery interrupted us.

I know she's gone to visit Shelly, because when I went back the next day to make sure she'd gotten a hold of her boyfriend, Shelly mentioned that Bryce had brought over a huge basket of stuff for her and the baby from the group at *Sportsverse*. Shelly named the baby Madden, which makes sense for a football fan, I guess.

Shelly said she didn't know who would be taking over for her in the interim, but that her boss said he would inform them to follow her lead, and that she'll be working with them to make sure the article we discussed still gets written about me. I told her not to worry about it, although I've been fixated on it ever since she gave birth. With Shelly on my side, I felt I didn't have to worry about what might appear in the article, but now with Bryce here, my stomach churns. I hope she's not Shelly's replacement.

"Everyone, sit down," Coach Iverson says once the players have all arrived. "Our GM Ronnie Michaels has an announcement to make, then I'm going to say a few words."

He steps back, and Ronnie Michaels takes the microphone.

"Why didn't she tell me?" Cooper mumbles, obviously assuming the same thing I am.

Ronnie says, "I just wanted to say we're off to a great start this season, and I hope this change will make it even better. Shelly Breckles from *Sportsverse* is our usual reporter for the team, and I know a lot of you formed relationships with her over the years since she's been our point person, but congratulations to her, she had a baby. And thanks to our own Miles Cavanaugh, she got to the hospital in time to give birth since she apparently didn't even know she was pregnant."

Cooper elbows me and winks as our other teammates whisper. Maybe they think I was kissing up to Shelly since I was with her at the time, or maybe they're talking about the fact that she didn't know she was pregnant. Or worse, I heard she was a bit of a flirt, maybe they think I was hanging out with her because there's something going on between us.

"Shelly's on maternity leave for the foreseeable future, and they've sent us a replacement. Let me introduce you to Bryce Burns, who is now the *Sportsverse* reporter for the Chicago Grizzlies. She'll be traveling with us to away games, and you'll see her in the locker room, requesting interviews from certain players. I don't have to remind you to treat her with respect." He signals for Bryce to say something.

She clears her throat. "Shelly is an excellent reporter, and I can only hope to fill her shoes. I will warn you though, she might have been a tad nicer than me. I write the truth, and yes, some of it is only my opinion, but you should know that while it may be tough, I'm always fair."

"Think you'd object to that comment, huh, Miles?" Damon whispers. But as usual, he's not that quiet.

Bryce looks at us. "I love football. I've been going to games with my dad since I was little, so I'm happy to be back reporting on my favorite sport. Go Grizzlies."

Everyone claps because she's in charge of how we're presented in the biggest magazine in the nation.

Coach Iverson takes the microphone from her. "Give Bryce a bigger welcome than that."

Everyone claps louder.

"Okay, Cavanaugh, you've been selected to give Miss Burns the tour of our facility." I must give him a look because Coach is quick to respond. "You two couldn't play nice in San Francisco, but you will do so here. The rest of you are done for the day. Don't be late for the plane tomorrow."

All the players file out and I walk down the stairs, taking my time.

"And here's your personal escort," Ronnie says. "Our very own Miles Cavanaugh."

"Hey," I say.

"Hi," she says.

"Okay, you two, let's not act like you're in high school. You're grown adults," Coach says.

"Come on." I open the side door and let Bryce file through first.

We say goodbye to Ronnie and Coach, and once we're on the other side of the door, she turns to me. "You don't have to show me around. I'll manage."

"Well, as you know, I follow the rules, so let's go."

I start walking, and she falls in line next to me. Her perfume wafts to my nostrils, and my dick twitches. If she's going to be around all the time now, I have to get myself under control and remember that she doesn't want anything to do with me. If she did, she wouldn't have walked out on me that morning, wouldn't look for an argument every chance she gets, and might have seemed receptive to my dinner invitation the other night.

I hate having her so close. It causes all the memories to resurface.

"So, this is the interview room." I step on the stage where the players sit. "We sit here, and you sit there." I point at the chairs on the other side of the table.

"Thanks. I've been in one before." She doesn't go to her chair.

"Should we practice you interrogating me?"

"That's not my job now. I get to observe and have full access to you and then write shitty things now." She raises her eyebrows.

I know she's trying to get a rise out of me, but all I can do is admire her shade of lipstick and think about how it draws my attention to her plump lips. Her dark hair is pinned up, showcasing her neck. I'd do just about anything right now to kiss her there, smell where her perfume has soaked into her skin.

"Great. I can't wait to be raked over the coals again. You

really do have a magic touch at making me look like the worst player in the league." I jump down from the stage and open the door for her to go first.

"If you continue playing how you have been, then I won't write anything bad." She slides her hands in the pockets of her slacks.

We walk down the hallway, and I open the locker room doors. The cleaning staff is picking up all our shit to be washed.

"Hey, Jack," I say to the guy in charge of making sure we have everything in our lockers for our games.

"Miles." He nods. "Did you try that chicken place I told you about?"

I laugh. "Not yet, but it's on my list."

"Best in Chicago," he adds.

"I see a lot of 'Best in Chicago.' The question remains: what's the best pizza place in this town?"

He wheels a bin of dirty towels forward, and another man takes it from him. "That depends on who you ask. You need to try every one and report back. Then I'll tell you my favorite."

"Deal." I wink. I don't tell him that it could take me six months to work my way through them all since I rarely cheat on my clean eating, especially during the season.

"I want in on this action," Bryce says, sticking her hand out to Jack. "I'm Bryce Burns with *Sportsverse Magazine.* I'm covering for Shelly Breckles while she's on maternity leave."

"Bryce, you're the mascot girl, no?" Jack asks, lowering his glasses as though he has to get a better look.

"I am. Sorry. That's just something my friend and I have done to Cooper since college. Obviously, that won't happen again." She gives him an innocent smile as if she's as sugary sweet as a sundae with three cherries on top.

I almost laugh out loud at the thought. She's about as sour as a lemon.

"I found it rather funny, but Coach didn't."

"I heard." She cringes then looks at me. "Cooper said he almost got benched."

"Coach wasn't pleased, but I don't think it would have come to that," I say.

"Nice to meet you, Bryce," Jack says. "Let me know if any of these guys get out of hand." He looks at me, and I hold up my hands.

"Believe me, you're more likely to have to protect me from her," I say.

He looks between us, the glasses still resting on the tip of his nose. "Huh. Better get to work. Big day tomorrow. Let me know on the pizza. There's one just down the street if you want to get started."

"I already had lunch." Bryce is quick to take that option off the table.

Jack nods. "I was just sayin', that's all."

He disappears out the door, and I point toward all the lockers. "Here's the locker room. You've met Jack, our equipment guy. Do you want to see the showers?"

"And envision all of you guys naked and comparing dick sizes?" She arches an eyebrow.

"As you're aware, I'm the winner in that department."

She scoffs and shakes her head.

I'm not usually a guy who'd make a comment like that. It's more of a Damon thing to say, but I want to push her off her axis. Why? I don't know.

"I'm not sure I remember that."

"Figures." I walk ahead of her, but her heels click until she's right next to me.

"I was joking, okay? Want me to say you have the biggest dick I've ever seen?" She whispers the last part presumably so no one will accidentally hear her.

We walk to some of the breakout rooms, then we're on the elevator so I can take her up to the front office.

"I don't need you to boost my ego. I'm confident about my dick size. I grew up in locker rooms. I know my worth in that department."

She blushes.

"Hard to forget, right?" I wink, and the elevator doors open.

"I forgot it the minute I walked out of your apartment."

She steps out of the elevator first, walking toward the front office where Ronnie's office is, along with media relations, human resources, and accounting.

"Keep telling yourself that." We pass a big cut-out of Cooper holding a razor. I gesture around. "This is the front office."

"It's nice." She stops and stares out the window. "It's so beautiful."

"What is?" I look at the sky. It's blue with a sparse number of clouds. There are birds flying around the empty stands in the stadium, looking for any scraps that the clean-up crew missed. One flies away with a popcorn kernel.

"The field. How green it is, the white lines marked perfectly, and the yellow goalposts. It just… brings up memories for me every time."

"Come on." I nod to keep going, and she takes one last look before she follows me.

"Where else is there to show me?" she asks.

"One more spot." We ride the elevator down to ground level and walk down the tunnel until we're at the edge of the field. "Have you ever been out there?"

She doesn't answer but steps onto the field, staring up at all the seats. "Never when it's been empty." She circles around. "It looks so much bigger."

I follow her, remaining quiet. She must really love football because she looks as in awe as I was the first time I stood on the fifty-yard line with no fans in attendance.

"I was thinking about what you said to me the other day

at the hospital… about everyone watching your every move, ready to comment on it. How do you do it? How do you play with so many eyes on you?"

She slips off her heels and walks onto the grass. Her toes are painted a cloudy blue color that gives away the fact that Bryce isn't always as serious as she might first appear. There's a fun side to her, just not a lot of people who get to see it.

"You get used to it."

She looks at me over her shoulder. "Do you?"

I shove my hands in my pockets. "I guess you get used to having to push it aside. Not have it be front and center in your mind the entire time you're out there."

"I can't imagine that's easy with everyone yelling and screaming." She stands at the fifty-yard line right where the coin toss takes place. "I might have a newfound respect for you."

I chuckle. "It took you being on an empty field?"

"It's the sheer massiveness of it. That on any game day, there's someone in all those seats, here to watch you. I can't fathom what that feels like."

"Is Bryce Burns being empathetic?" I ask, earning a glare then a laugh.

"Don't tell anyone." She circles around. "I wish we had a ball."

"Maybe one day," I say, sounding more wistful than I want to.

She shrugs and inhales. "I want to remember this forever."

"I'm sure Cooper can get you on the field any time you want."

She doesn't say anything and turns toward me, her face softer, kinder. "Do you want to try the pizza place Jack suggested?"

My eyebrow arches. "I thought you already had lunch?"

"I lied. I need to write a story for this week's column. Want to be my subject?"

"I'm not sure."

"It's my treat. Or *Sportsverse's* actually."

"Well in that case, I can't turn it down."

Without warning, she runs down the field, squealing in delight before she stops, spinning around with her arms out. It's a side of Bryce I've never really seen, and it doesn't take a genius to know that probably very few people have.

I like it. I like this less inhibited, softer side of this woman.

I meet her over by her shoes, and she's catching her breath when she approaches. "Sorry, I had to get it out of my system."

"It was the best show this field's ever seen."

Our gazes collide, and she opens her mouth to say something but seems to think better of it. "Let's go."

She offered me a peek through the window into who she is, but as usual, she slammed the shutters closed before I could get a good look.

CHAPTER 11

BRYCE

Mr. Osterman stands next to me while we watch the Chicago Grizzlies practice. He demanded that he come with me on my first day, which I hate because it makes me feel as though I brought my daddy to work with me.

They're running drills with the running backs and wide receivers. Cooper looks great out of the pocket.

"So, I talked with Shelly earlier this morning, and she wasn't aware that you were so close with the guys who live in The Den."

I look at him from the corner of my eye. "The Den?"

"You didn't know? The place where Cooper, Damon, and Miles live. It's always had Grizzlies players in and out of there, and of course, a lot of women have made their way through there as well. They refer to it as The Den." He laughs, but I don't find it funny.

"How endearing. That has to be Damon's doing."

Speak of the devil, the man makes a great catch in the end zone and sticks out his tongue as he runs by me, saying something about how great he is. That man's ego is way too inflated for his own good.

"I think Creed started the nickname actually. You know he retired last year."

Who does he think he's talking to? As if I wouldn't know about Creed's retirement. He was one of the best tight ends in the league. He had the reputation of having a revolving door of women, but that's not unlike a lot of professional athletes.

"Yeah, I'm aware. So, Miles took his spot."

"Yep."

"I'd bet that Cooper Rice and Miles Cavanaugh don't refer to their place as The Den, nor do I think they'll have women in and out of there. Now, Damon I can't really speak for."

Miles is on the sidelines, talking with the defensive coach and getting ready to come in. I can't wait to see him in action. He really has improved his game this season.

"I don't know. When players start making a name for themselves, and getting recognized by more than just diehard fans, they change. I wouldn't put it past either of them to start bringing women home, plus with Damon there…"

For the life of me, I have no idea why we're talking about The Den when my articles will be about them as players.

"Doubtful, but I guess you never know." Coming from a girl with a father who was never satisfied with just one woman, I can't really say it with finality.

"Anyway, Shelly really wants to stay abreast of what you're writing and what you're learning in interviews, so I figure a weekly meeting. Just so when she returns, she's not lost."

His reminder that this position is only temporary sits like spoiled milk in my stomach. I better prove myself here so I can get in with another national team.

"Okay." I don't much like the idea of giving Shelly all my notes. The last thing I want is her dictating the tone of my articles and what I should explore.

"Don't think much of it. She's just working on a more in-depth piece for the end of the season. You have complete say in your weekly articles."

I nod, jotting down notes on the players I'm watching and what they're doing that I think will help the team this year. "Sure."

He claps when Damon and Miles are head-to-head on a ball Cooper throws to the end zone. Both of them miss it and it bounces out toward the stands. Miles jogs to get it and throws it to the coach. He shakes his head at himself.

"Cavanaugh always that hard on himself?" Mr. Osterman asks me.

"From what I've seen, he is. I think he's kind of a perfectionist."

He blows out a breath and rears back. "You can't be a perfectionist and a professional athlete. You'll constantly feel like you're a failure."

I agree with my boss. But before I can say that, Ronnie Michaels walks over, and I stare at his bare feet for a moment, thinking I'm seeing things, but nope. Khaki pants, an orange polo, and bare feet. Interesting look for the team's general manager.

"Billy Boy," he says to Mr. Osterman, who sticks out his hand for a handshake and manly hug where they compete for who can pat the other's back harder.

"Ronnie, the team looks amazing. I was just telling Bryce here how we should do an article on you and your ability to put together winning teams."

Um... no, he wasn't, but I smile and nod anyway. I hate lying, but this is my job, my livelihood. "He was."

"You're too kind. But I did work hard. Grabbing Cavanaugh last year was just the start, then we got lucky with those draft picks."

"I was going to ask what you were thinking, taking a safety in the fifth round when you just got Miles."

Mr. Osterman stiffens beside me and gives me a side-eye. I

guess they just want a pretty face to stand here and shove rainbows up their asses for them to shit out later.

"Never mind—"

"No, it's a great question, but I'd like my answer to be off the record," Ronnie says.

I move my pen away from my notebook.

"Our second string safety has a knee problem. I'm not sure he'll make the season without surgery. He's trying to delay it until the off-season, but we're not sure what will happen. Plus, you know Cavanaugh."

I school my features. Miles is way better on his off days than that kid they drafted. In fact, the kid should really be a cornerback, not a safety, but I keep my opinion to myself because I like my job and don't want to be fired on my first day covering the Grizzlies. "I guess that's why you're so brilliant."

"Now that stays between us, you hear me?" He laughs, a throaty, husky one that sounds like he's a three-pack-a-day smoker.

"I promise," I say.

"And don't tempt my players, BB," Ronnie says, looking right at me.

"Of course not," Mr. Osterman quickly responds.

My eyebrows damn near hit my hairline. "Excuse me?"

"You're an attractive woman. Young. Sometimes the play-ers... well, you know."

I want to say I don't and force him to enlighten me, but I know exactly what he's saying.

"I gave the same warning to Shelly when she came onboard. Not sure she understood," Ronnie says.

"Well, Bryce here is the consummate professional."

My attention is momentarily drawn to the field where Miles schools Damon, picking the ball off right before it hits his hands. Damon falls to his knees and screams, then jogs back to do the play all over again.

"Is that right? Good for her then." Ronnie puts out his hand. "Good to see you, Billy Boy, and BB, I'll be seeing you around."

I wave.

After Ronnie's a good distance away, pretending to box a player with a few jabs to the abdomen, Mr. Osterman clears his throat. "You'll have to go along with the BB thing the same as I do with Billy Boy."

"I know. Not the most unique, but I'll be fine. I know who allows us access to the team. No worries, Mr. Osterman."

He nods like a proud dad. "That's why I like you, Bryce. You get it. You'll do great here."

"I hope so."

"Just make sure that whatever relationship you have with Miles and Cooper, you keep it out of your articles. Don't let them off easy because they're your friends."

I hold my notepad to my chest and turn to face him. "I've known Cooper since college, but I'm not friends with Miles. We were in the same social circle back in San Francisco, and I had no problem conveying the player I thought he was, so you have no worries there."

"I'm glad." He glances at his old-school metal watch. "I'm gonna head back to the office. You're fine here?"

"I am." I nod. "I'll keep you updated on my article for this week."

"Perfect." His eyes widen, and his arms reach toward me, but I'm plowed over by a large body, taken down to the grass. "Bryce, are you okay?"

I look up from the grass, and the reflection off Mr. Osterman's bald head blinds me. I put my hand over my eyes. "I think so."

"Shit, I'm sorry, Bryce." Miles. Fucking Miles's voice. "My bad. I didn't see you standing there."

I accept his hand and stand, then look down at my grass-stained ivory pantsuit. "You really didn't see me?"

I don't buy it at all.

"I was so worried about getting the ball." He spins the ball in the air. He doesn't look apologetic in the least.

"You okay?" Mr. Osterman asks.

Even though my ankle is killing me, I nod. I must've twisted it or something when Miles ran into me. "I'm good. Please don't let me hold you up."

The sports physician comes over with his first aid kit, not even glancing over at me. "Everyone okay here? Miles, did you hurt yourself?"

"Um… he's, like, two hundred thirty pounds of pure muscle. I'm five-three and mostly made of carbs."

Miles laughs.

"Yes, ma'am." He must be an intern or something because he looks so young. "Are you hurt at all?"

"Honestly, my ankle hurts."

"Oh, that's not good," the kid says, staring down as though it should be turned the other way if it's hurting. "I'll take a look at it."

I'm not sure of this kid's qualifications, but Miles must read my mind because he squats down in front of me.

"What are you doing?" I ask.

"I'm taking you into the sports med office. Dr. Calvin can help you."

"You want to give me a piggyback ride?"

"Would you rather I pick you up bride style? I mean, if you want to pretend it's our wedding night, I'm game."

The kid's eyebrows furrow.

"You should go get checked out," Mr. Osterman says.

I climb onto Miles's back. "Keep your smartass comments to yourself," I murmur so just he can hear.

He laughs and stands to his full height, his arms hooking around my legs. After a quick goodbye to my boss, he heads off toward the tunnel.

"If I kick you, will you go faster?" I ask.

"If you kick me, I'll buck you off."

"Duly noted. It's on the record that you hit me at practice."

"I didn't see you." He's so serious, it makes me laugh.

Once we're in the tunnel and alone, I inhale Miles's scent. I can't help myself. He's sweaty but still smells fresh somehow. The ends of his dark hair are damp with sweat, and his back is hot beneath me. Memories of that night surface, my fingers feeling the dampness and sheen to his skin from the exertion of thrusting in and out of me or holding me against the wall as he drilled into me over and over again.

"I'm just joking. Thanks for the ride."

When we reach the physician's area, he sets me gently on an exam table. "Dr. Calvin, we have an injury."

A man with glasses resting on the tip of his nose and a head full of gray hair comes out of his office. He examines the situation and quickly figures out it's me. "You hurt her on her first day?" He slips off my shoe.

"And he ruined my pantsuit."

The doctor shakes his head and looks at Miles. "Bull in a china shop, huh?"

We all laugh, and Miles bites the inside of his lip. He shifts his weight from side to side.

"Go, Miles, I'll be fine," I say.

His forehead wrinkles.

"Go back to practice. Dr. Calvin will take care of me. I'll be fine."

"Are you sure? I can stay."

This is a part of Miles that I love, the kind and considerate side of him.

"I'm fine."

He sighs. "I'll see you after practice then." He steps forward as though he might kiss me or something, but then turns and jogs out of the room.

I'm lying down ten minutes later, icing my ankle, when

the kid from the medical team comes in. He hands me a vanilla and chocolate swirl cone.

"This is from Miles," he says.

I wish I could fight the smile on my face, but Miles is making me feel like a little kid. I got a boo-boo, so he got me an ice cream. Damn that man, sometimes he's too hard to resist.

"Smart man," Dr. Calvin says.

I lick the ice cream cone and nod.

He sure is.

CHAPTER 12
MILES

Our away game sucked. To clarify, *we* sucked. We were projected to win, but it all went to hell pretty quickly. The worst part about losing on the road is that we're all stuck with one another and the pissed off coaches on the flight home.

I open the book I brought with me. I've only just started it because I've had a hard time concentrating as of late. I read the first line as someone slides into the seat next to me. I glance over because whoever it is, didn't hit my shoulder and smells pretty fucking fantastic. Sure enough, it's Bryce.

She huffs and glances at me as she bends over and digs into her bag. "Believe me, I'd rather be anywhere but here. I boarded late, and this was the last seat."

"Ask the captain. Maybe you can sit in the cockpit, or perhaps they can rig something up on the wing."

"Haha, aren't you funny? Let's remember, no one else wanted to sit next to you. That's why the seat is open." She gives me a look to suggest she just schooled me.

"It's because I'm a reader. I don't sleep on planes. Everyone else will be out, and my light bothers them." I hold up the book as proof.

She glances up at the light and back down. Doesn't say anything and grabs the notebook she's always writing in out of her bag. "You know they have these cool things called e-readers with a backlight now?"

"You don't say. I'm an avid reader, and here I thought books only came in paperback."

"It was just a helpful hint, so you don't have to sit by yourself." She writes something in her notebook.

"Thanks for the tip, but I enjoy sitting by myself."

She rocks her head back then nods. "You are kind of a loner."

"Being okay alone is not the same as being a loner." I straighten my back, adjust my light, and open my book. Hopefully she understands that's my nonverbal way of telling her the conversation is over.

"You know what you did wrong tonight, right?" she says after a minute has passed.

Here we go. "I'll wait for you to pick me apart in your article, thanks."

"I'm serious. Porter juked you out, and it's because you're not watching his hips, you're just watching his upper body. You assumed he was going right, but his hips gave him away."

"In case you missed it, I've been playing the position for years now."

"Well, I think you're forgetting some of the basics."

I shut my book, take off my reading glasses, and turn my body toward her, crossing my arms. "Want to do drills with me sometime?"

She mimics my body language. "I'd love to."

The worst part is she's right. I knew the minute Porter got by. It's 101 shit, and I didn't do it.

"You all had a bad game, so—"

"So you're excusing me for fucking the team over?" I relax my arms as the pilot announces we're going to take off.

She leans in close, and her long hair brushes my arm. "Did you miss Coop's three interceptions? You're hardly the one to be blamed for this loss."

"It doesn't matter what other people do. It's what I did, and I failed them."

She shakes her head and pushes back into her seat when the plane rushes down the runway. Then her hands grip the armrest, and she closes her eyes. I take the opportunity to watch her without her knowing.

Her long dark hair is curled into ringlets. Her makeup only makes her natural beauty shine a little brighter. The pink of her lipstick makes it look like she just licked her lips. She's not the girl next door type. She's sexy and confident and appealing. The minute I saw her all those years ago, put a face to the woman who was calling me out in the *Chronicle*, I almost couldn't believe it.

Since Bryce can be either a man or woman's name, I'd assumed she was a cranky old man with teeth stained yellow from drinking coffee from sunup to sundown. Someone who liked old-school players and ate meat and potatoes every night. Thought someone like me, a healthy eater with his green smoothies and a sometimes-vegetarian diet, wasn't a real man and only real men should play football.

Then she came to the Kingsmen, and I saw her in real life on the sidelines. It was all over for me.

She exhales a long breath, tearing me out of my memory. Her knuckles are white, and her chest rises with a big inhale.

"Are you scared to fly?" I whisper.

"No," she snaps.

"Then why are you gripping the armrest like you're hanging off the edge of a cliff?"

She peeks one eye open. "Maybe a little. I don't like takeoff and turbulence."

"You know it's a control thing, right?"

She peeks one eye open again and shuts it. "Just go about

what you're doing. I've done this enough times to get through it."

"Do you want to hold my hand?" I hold out my palm.

"No." She opens her eyes and shoos me away before locking her hand back on the armrest.

"Are you sure? It might make you feel better."

She moves her hand again, but the plane dips, and her eyes squeeze shut. Her hand falls in mine, or I hijack it, I'm not sure which, but the result is the same. I grab a hold of her, and she squeezes it, reminding me of Shelly when she was giving birth.

"Give me a little circulation," I whisper, but a quick glance around the plane cabin shows me everyone is falling asleep. There are no other lights on.

I turn off my light with my free hand and tuck my book in the pocket of the seat in front of me. The pilot comes on and says it's going to be a choppy flight, and that he'll be keeping the seatbelt sign on for the duration of the flight. The plane dips a few more times, and she continues to squeeze my hand.

I admire our hands linked together. Her small one encased in my big calloused one. It's silly, but it makes me wonder what might have happened if she'd acted differently after our night together two years ago. What if we were a couple? We wouldn't be sitting here. She wouldn't be writing about me because that'd be a clear conflict of interest. Hell, maybe she'd still be in San Francisco at her old job and wouldn't have followed me here.

The option of our relationship one day turning romantic has passed. There's too much at stake now. Her career being the biggest one. I know how important it is to her, and she'd never want to be known for messing around with an athlete she's reporting on, and I would never ask her to do that. It was different in San Francisco. Now she's at a national level sports magazine. You can't just snap your fingers and go find another job like that.

Her head falls against my shoulder and the flowery scent of her shampoo floats up to my nose. My brain understands what's at stake. Now I just need my dick to as well.

———

The plane's tires land on the runway, and Bryce jolts awake. She looks over at me and swallows audibly. Then her vision shifts around the plane, where most players are just waking up as well. She was so peaceful as she slept with her head on my shoulder, I couldn't wake her.

"Oh my god," she whispers to herself, staring at the wet spot on my shirt from her drool. "Why did you let me sleep? On you?" Her eyes widen, and I'm not sure she wants my real answer, so I play it off.

"Next time, should I refuse to let my shoulder be your pillow?" I unbuckle my seat belt and grab my book, shoving it in my backpack while I turn my phone off Airplane Mode. She does the same, but hers dings a bunch of times, whereas mine is silent.

"It's surprisingly comfortable."

"Good to know. I'll make sure to put that on my dating profile. 'Shoulder is surprisingly comfortable for naps on planes.'"

She giggles, and my ego boosts a bit because I brought that out of her.

"You're not on a dating site, are you?" I'm not sure of the expression I give, but she chuckles. "I just meant—"

"Does it make you jealous? Thinking of me with someone else?"

I'm not sure of the answer I want. I spent the entire trip back to Chicago listing all the reasons we can't be together, and now I'm baiting her to say she feels jealous where I'm concerned.

"No," she says. "I just meant it's not exactly like you need a dating site."

The plane is taxiing, and most of the team is collecting their stuff. Damon's razzing Cooper about his interceptions, and Cooper's pointing out all his flaws during the game. No one is paying attention to us, so I figure I'm not going to hold back.

"So, you're saying I'm attractive?"

She looks at me from the corner of her eye, her notebook giving her trouble as she tries over and over to shove it into her bag. "I'm pretty sure you know you're attractive. Have you never looked in a mirror?"

"Well, my shoulders are surprisingly comfortable. Maybe you also think my jaw is surprisingly chiseled? That my lips are surprisingly full and soft? My eyes so surprisingly clear you could lose yourself in them?"

"Are you done fishing for compliments? Do you need me to stroke your ego a bit so you can gain enough confidence to hit on a woman at a bar?" She finally gets the notebook in her bag, and she zips it up. I would've helped, but she would've hated me for it.

My face screws up. "The last place I'd pick up a woman is a bar."

"Why?"

"Because they're only out to say they slept with me. That's not what I'm looking for."

"And what are you looking for?" She glances around to double-check that no one's paying attention to us.

"Someone I can dedicate my life to. A wife, the kids, the dog, the house. I want it all."

She's giving me a look like maybe she thinks I'm crazy. "Right now, you want all that?"

It'd be nice, but I'm not sure if it's destined to happen. "I do. But although I have a decent off-season, football season is hard, and you have to be one hundred percent committed. I don't want a wife worrying about me out there. Not that I would ever cheat, but it's hard to be the wife of a player in the league. Takes a special kind of woman to deal with all of that. If I can find a woman who can deal with that while I'm still in the league, perfect. But I realize it might have to wait until I'm done playing. I've seen marriages crash and burn after months, or only last only a season or two. The happy ones are few and far between."

"That's not true. Look at Lee and Shayna, Brady and Violet. Look at your sister and Chase. They're all making it work." She ticks them off on her fingers.

She has a point I guess.

"True." I shrug. "Maybe I just haven't met 'the one' yet then."

She sucks in a sharp breath and says nothing. The flight attendants open the cabin door, and all the players rise out of their seats to file out, so our conversation ends there. Once we're off the plane, she shoulders through the crowd before I can catch up to her.

At the car riding line, she's with Cooper, and both of them have their phones out. I'm thinking the messages coming through are from Ellery, but I don't really know.

Damon comes up alongside me. "Share a ride back to our place?" He claps me on the shoulder.

My eyes remain on Bryce as she heatedly talks with Cooper. What am I missing?

"It's not our place," I say.

He laughs. "Don't be so literal." He elbows me. "Saw you had your 'girl wonder' next to you. Any kissing while everyone was asleep?"

"She's not my 'girl wonder.' She's the reporter for the team."

He leans in close. "I see the way you look at her, man. Your secret is safe with me."

I shake my head as my car arrives. I can't get in it fast enough. Unfortunately, Damon slides in right next to me. The driver pulls off the curb, and we drive farther and farther away from where Bryce stands.

How can I miss her already? I only ever get small bits of time with her. What I wouldn't do for a chunk of time, a meal, anything. Once again, I have to remind myself of all the reasons why we can't be together. Probably the biggest of which is that she doesn't want to be with me. She ran out on me—I should tattoo it on my skin, so I don't forget.

CHAPTER 13

BRYCE

"You need to answer your mom. She called me while you were on the plane," Elle continues her lecture to me on the phone.

I blow out a breath. "I'm not talking to her right now. I can't. She's being so stupid. What is she thinking, taking him back?"

I hear the sound of someone at the hospital speaking over the intercom.

"It's her decision, not yours. You need to support her." Elle uses her sweet voice. The one she'll probably use when she's a mother and her kid scrapes his knee. It's part of what makes her a great doctor—her excellent bedside manner and ability to deliver difficult information with a calming voice.

"It's my decision not to involve myself in it. He's going to hurt her again."

All I hear is her breathing for a moment. "You're so stubborn."

"You know I have my reasons." Elle, out of everyone, knows the hang-ups my dad left me with.

When your parents divorce when you're young, and every time you're with your dad he leaves you in a hotel room to go pick up some random woman, you tend to grow up with hang-ups. My mom got sick a few years ago, and my dad returned home to help, and shortly after, they called to tell me that they'd fallen back in love. And now they're getting married and want me to stand by their sides as they celebrate their love on some beach in Jamaica.

I'm so thankful my mom is in remission, but I cannot pretend to be happy that she wants to remarry my father.

"It doesn't sound like your dad is who he was before."

"Right now, he isn't. What about years down the road when he forgets what he felt like when he thought she was going to die, and he's no longer satisfied with her? He tossed her to the curb once, he'll do it again."

"Okay, I have to go back to my patients, my five minutes are up. I'm not getting through to you at all anyway. So, drinks tomorrow?"

"Maybe. I have to go meet with Shelly Breckles today, then I'm on my article for this week. If I get enough done, sure."

"The girl who didn't know she was pregnant? Isn't she on maternity leave?" Her tone is judgmental, and I assume it's because she's in the medical field and can't fathom someone not knowing they're pregnant, but some people aren't in tune with their bodies.

"Yeah, it's a long story, I'll tell you when I see you."

"Okay. Love you. Think about the advice your wise friend just gave you. Plus, if your mom calls me again, I'm adding you to the call. Gotta go."

She hangs up before I can stop her. I'll have to be careful when I answer her phone calls from now on.

I head to the L train station and follow the directions that Shelly gave me on the phone.

As I sit on the train and do one of my favorite things—people watch—I go over what my options are for the article. I have no choice but to be truthful about how the Grizzlies played, but I can't imagine showing my face at the stadium if I trash them in print. I'm going to have to finesse my words.

My thoughts drift to Miles and the fact that I drooled on his shoulder. He held my hand the whole plane ride, and I can't remember the last time I allowed myself to be vulnerable like that with someone. But it felt nice to have someone take some of the weight from me.

I get off the L and walk the three blocks to Bucktown. She lives in an apartment on the second floor of a four-flat. She buzzes me up, and I hear the baby crying the entire way up the stairs. I knock softly even though the baby is awake.

Shelly answers the door with her hair pulled up in a messy bun, her freckled skin on display in her tank top and shorts.

"Hey, come on in." She steps aside, rocking the baby who is still crying. "Would you mind taking him?"

She shoves the baby wrapped in a blue blanket into my arms before I can answer. I lower my one shoulder so my messenger bag falls to the floor while she walks over to the kitchen.

"He's been needy all day. Do you want a drink?"

I'm relieved when she pulls out a bottle of water. For some reason, I assumed she meant a drink *drink*. Although it's really none of my business. I don't even know if she's breast-feeding.

"I'm okay. Mr. Osterman said you wanted me to share information with you?"

Her eyes light up. "Actually, first, I want to hear how you know Cooper Rice so well."

She moves from the kitchen over to the couch and sits cross-legged as I hold her baby, who finally stops crying. I'm not really a baby kind of person. I love them, think they're cute, but I'm an only child. If it wasn't for Elle and her big family, I wouldn't even know what it's like to be around kids.

"Um." I sit on the edge of the chair across from her,

glancing at the bassinet and hoping she'll tell me to put him in there, but I think since he's not crying, this is how I'll spend my time here. "I went to college with him."

"And your friend Ellery, are they dating?" She's not asking like she's making conversation, more like she's conducting an interview. Actually, more of an interrogation.

"No, they're just friends." I keep all my thoughts about them to myself. Shelly doesn't need to know that.

"And Damon, you know him?"

I shake my head. "No, I only met him when I arrived in town."

"Okay, then you knew Miles from San Francisco, right?"

I nod then tilt my head.

"You were friends with him there?"

"Shelly, can I ask why you want to know all this?"

She draws back, seeming surprised. "I'm just curious to see how close you are to the subjects. Grant mentioned it."

"Well, I can assure you, as I did him, that my personal feelings aren't going to be incorporated in my articles. They won't get a free pass." I fiddle with the baby's pacifier.

"I didn't think that, but I'm interested to see your article this week after that terrible game they had."

"Yeah, I was thinking on the way over about how I would handle it." I tell her what I'm thinking, and we go back and forth for a few minutes.

Then we sit in silence, and she watches me with her son. All I want to do is pass him back and get out of here. I see no sign of her boyfriend, and it's the middle of the day. Aren't chefs usually home during the day and out at dinner?

"Where's your boyfriend?" I ask just to break the silence.

"He's out grocery shopping. He's been a big help."

"That's great."

"Uh-huh."

We sit in silence for another minute until finally she comes over and takes the baby, then places him in his bassinet.

"Thanks for getting him to fall asleep," she says.

"I'm not sure I did anything."

"Can I see your notes?"

I want to grab my bag, hug it to my chest in toddler fashion, and shake my head, repeating no, over and over again. But she's just looking out for her job, making sure things are okay in her absence. If I want to get assigned to another national team at some point, I have to play nice with the others. Mr. Osterman was clear that I had to share everything with her, so I hand her my notebook.

She flips through the pages, reading it with no facial expressions. The longer she's quiet, the more worried I become. Finally, she places it on the table between us. "You're very observant."

"Thanks."

"Looks like you have things handled. Good luck on this week's article. I want to shower while he's sleeping, so we'll meet up next week, okay?" She stands and grabs the baby monitor sitting on the coffee table.

By the time I stand, she's halfway to the hallway.

"Sure, okay."

I walk toward the door, and I notice all her heels in a pile by the door. I imagine that when you have a baby, you have no time to do anything else, like put your shoes away.

When the door shuts behind me, I've never felt freer in my life. My reporter gut is telling me something is going on, but I can't figure out what.

———

The article wasn't received as badly as I expected. Cooper told me the locker room understood they'd played a crappy game and didn't have any hard feelings toward me.

It was a home game this week, so Elle and I decided to wait for the guys at the stadium. Sometimes it's fun to watch the jersey-chasers in action. But the weather is changing fast, and it's colder at night. Something I didn't dress for, so I shiver uncontrollably.

"Where the hell is he? Take a shower and get out here, Coop." I shake my head as Elle laughs.

"I get that you lived in San Francisco for a while, but what were you thinking, not bringing a jacket with you?" She's using her judgmental, oldest-child voice with me.

"Because I'm not used to grabbing a jacket on the way out the door this time of year. The weather is so unpredictable here." I wrap my arms around myself, and my teeth chatter.

The doors finally open.

"Thank fuck," I murmur quietly, since there are some kids with parents waiting.

Damon walks out, and he high fives, signs autographs, and winks at the women. All the women wearing short dresses corral around him as though he's the stud and they'll happily sign up to take turns.

"I'm nauseated watching him," I say.

"Yeah, it's annoying. He probably won't be coming back to Coop's tonight. If he does, he's going to bring one of them." Elle's nose wrinkles.

The doors open again, and my heart lodges in my throat when it's Miles and a few other defensive players. He's wearing a suit, although not all players wear them out. His broad shoulders in the navy-blue jacket with a classic white shirt and no tie look phenomenal. The shirt is tucked into his taut waist, and he's got brown shoes paired with it. But it's the blue of his suit pulling out the color in his eyes, contrasting with his dark hair, that really gets my heart racing.

He has a duffel bag swung over his shoulder, and the women who Damon isn't giving any attention to turns to him.

"Miles!" they call in unison.

"If I thought I was nauseous before, I'm literally swallowing bile back down now."

Elle glances at me but says nothing. I already know her thoughts. I don't need to read her mind.

Miles walks over to the women, and I watch his every step, wanting to run over there and take those girls by their hair, swing them around, and shot put them right into Lake Michigan like shot puts.

"He was just telling me last night, he doesn't..." I stop talking because he walks right past them and kneels in front of the kids.

"Aw..." Elle puts her hand over her heart. "I love it when Coop does that."

I feel her eyes on me, but I refuse to give her any reaction. She'll read into it.

Of course, subtlety doesn't run through Elle's veins, so she elbows me as if I'm not purposefully ignoring her. "See, they're not all bad."

I ignore her. Cooper comes out a few minutes later and gives some high fives, a few autographs to the parents and kids, but he ignores the women as well before he's right in front of us.

"I didn't know you guys were waiting for me," he says in a tone that suggests it's a problem.

I really hope he doesn't have a date or something. Elle will pretend she doesn't care, but then she'll ask me questions all night like, "what do you think his type is?" or "where do you think he took her?" I'm not in the mood to deal with it when I'm trying to shelter myself from probing questions at the moment.

"We said we were going to," Elle says.

"Well, bad news. I drove the Corvette today. Two-seater."

Cooper has an old-school Corvette that he restored with his dad a long time ago. He doesn't take it out of storage a lot, so I'm curious why he did today.

"My dad's birthday," he says without us asking. Cooper isn't one to hide much.

"Well, you go and I'll Uber it," Elle is quick to say to me.

"No need. We have two more guys who are going to the same place. Miles!" he yells.

Miles finishes signing the last kid's hat and takes a picture with him before walking over. He gives me a once-over, and as cold as I am, I feel as if I just stepped in front of a bonfire for a moment the way his gaze drags over me. His bag drops to the ground, and he shrugs out of his suit jacket, handing it over to me.

"Aw," Ellery says way too loudly.

"I'm fine," I say.

"Take the jacket, Bryce," he says with a bite to his tone.

"Fine. Thanks." I sound begrudging, and he shakes his head at me.

"Can you get Bryce back to our place?" Cooper asks.

"I'm a grown woman, I can Uber."

"Well, we'll share one. Mine is already here." He nods toward the car waiting at the edge of the parking lot.

"I can get there myself," I argue, but Elle and Cooper are already walking over to his Corvette.

Mile sighs. "Just get in the car, Bryce."

I huff and follow because what choice do I have? Now I'm wearing his suit jacket and riding with him back to his place in the same Uber. To an outsider, it looks as though we're dating. That's the last thing I need.

CHAPTER 14

MILES

"You didn't tell me he was coming," Bryce says loudly enough for me to hear.

Ellery and Cooper planned for us to go tubing on some river an hour outside of the city. She even rented a big SUV so we could all travel together.

"I assumed you were coming. It's no one's fault you didn't do the same." I toss my backpack in the back of the vehicle.

Bryce is wearing a T-shirt that's so threadbare that I know she's wearing a bikini because I can see the outline of her bikini top through the fabric, even if the strings around her neck didn't give it away. Her cutoff jean shorts only enhance her appeal, showing off her sexy legs.

Damn it all to hell. Maybe I should cut my losses and bail on this thing.

"We're all going. Even Damon's..." Ellery doesn't finish her sentence because Damon doesn't do labels and probably has no idea how to refer to his latest fling.

"Her name is Mika, and I'd like you all to behave nicely toward her." Damon walks over to the Uber that just pulled up on the curb.

He opens the back door, and a woman with long legs, big

breasts, her hair in a ponytail, steps out. She's wearing a bikini with a very small amount of fabric and a see-through cover-up. Let's just say Damon knows how to pick them.

"Shit," Bryce says. "She's stunning. How does he get these women?"

"Now I have to keep my shirt on all day. I haven't been to the gym in weeks because I've had back-to-back shifts." Ellery's eyes remain on Mika.

"You are both hot as fuck. Stop comparing yourselves to other women." Cooper grabs the keys from Ellery. "Let's go."

We all file into the SUV. Damon and his girl are in the far back, Bryce and me in the middle, and Ellery in the passenger seat next to Cooper. The hour-long drive is filled with Cooper and Ellery trying to act like a mom and dad, wanting us to play games or do a stupid sing-along, while the rest of us act like teenagers, ignoring them with our heads buried in our phones.

When we finally arrive at our destination, we pull down the gravel drive, Cooper following the signs to the tubing river. A lot of families and groups of people are already getting out of their cars and putting on sunscreen by their vehicles. We park farther in the back because we'd like to do this without being recognized if we can.

Cooper, Damon, and I put on ball caps and sunglasses, but our big frames sometimes draw attention and give us away. Hopefully, not today, since from what I researched, we're on our own rafting, not in an assigned group. We just have to get through the safety class, and then we're good.

But all the research I did—the river shoes I bought, the sunscreen, bug spray, and even a waterproof bag to put my phone in—didn't prepare me for Bryce taking off her T-shirt.

Her narrow waist and more-than-a-handful tits tugging on the sand-colored fabric of her bikini make my mouth hang open. I probably look like a thirsty dog after a long walk with my tongue hanging out the side, panting. As if she's trying to torture me, she unbuckles her jean shorts and shimmies them down her legs, her ass in my face until she steps out of them.

"Stick your tongue back in your mouth," Damon whispers and smacks me on the back.

Bryce turns around, and I quickly look in the other direction, pretending I wasn't gawking at her.

I put on my sunscreen, and although I would've done it, Ellery puts Bryce's sunblock on her back.

"Elle, I'll do you if you do me," Cooper says.

"Damon, spray my back," I say.

He narrows his eyes. "Ask Bryce."

She hurriedly buries her head in her bag as if she's searching for something. I approach her because I really don't have a choice, and it's a spray, not a lotion, anyway.

"Would you mind?" I hold it out to her.

"Oh." Her eyes meet mine, and my heart leaps. "Sure."

I turn around and hold out my arms. She sprays it then massages it in. It's almost impossible to ignore how good her hand feels roaming over my skin. I have to think about dead puppies and my parents having sex not to get a hard-on.

"This way you're completely covered. You don't want weird lines," she says.

I nod, trying to appear unaffected. "Thanks."

After the awkward moment has passed, Damon hikes Mika up on his back and leads the pack toward the rafts.

Cooper comes alongside me. "Think he's gonna give us away?"

"If he does, then we leave him." I'm serious, but Cooper laughs as if I'm not.

I've known Damon a long time, and he's a great guy. Definitely a friend who would be there for you, but he's loud and loves to be the life of the party. I'm pretty sure it's a facade to a degree, but I only know that from one drunken night in college when he opened up about his past. But it was only bits and pieces, and I could never piece it all together.

We go through the safety class, grab our tubes, and head to the river.

It's a free-for-all, so Damon puts Mika in a raft, pushes hers out, then pushes his off and jumps in, almost tipping it. All I hear is his laugh as he ventures down the river.

Cooper waits for Ellery to get in a raft before he gets in his own.

"You got B, right, Miles?" Cooper asks, spinning Ellery around, who squeals.

"Don't worry, I can handle it myself." Bryce puts her raft in the water, stands on the rock, and falls back into the opening, floating away.

Not wanting to be the last one, I do the same.

We travel down the river, talking about nothing much at all. Damon and Mika are so far ahead that they're on their own, leaving it just the four of us. Ellery and Bryce talk about some show they're watching while Cooper and I discuss our upcoming game.

The girls eventually stop talking and seem content to sunbathe in the raft with their heads tipped back and eyes closed. I hit a rock and my float stops, which they warned us about during the safety orientation. I use my feet to get free, but it slows me down enough that I'm behind the group. Then I see that Bryce has floated into an inlet that isn't pushing her back out.

"B!" Ellery calls, as she and Cooper continue to flow down the river.

Bryce opens her eyes and looks around. "Oh my god! Wait for me, Elle!" She laughs.

"I got you," I say and switch positions to be on my stomach so I can paddle over to her.

"I can do it." She shimmies to the end of the raft for her feet to go in and push her out, but the raft pops out from under her and she ends up in the river.

Ellery's laugh rings out, but I'm not even sure it's because of Bryce since they're so far ahead.

"Here." I hold out my hand.

"Stop trying to save me all the time."

I retract my hand. "Fine. I'll leave it to you. See you at the end."

I push forward and she stands on the rock, grabbing the inner tube and trying to get back in it, but she slips on the rocks and falls forward, the raft sliding out from under her.

"You sure?" I arch an eyebrow.

Her anger is like fire in her eyes, but she sighs. "Fine. But seriously…"

"Seriously what? I'm just helping you like I would anyone else. Doesn't make you special." The words taste sour on my tongue.

She frowns as I hold her raft in place for her to get on it. "I just… forget it. Thanks."

I'm not going to press her for more information. I probably wouldn't like what she had to say anyway.

Just as we get back on track, one drop of rain falls onto the water, then a few more, until suddenly it's pouring.

"Why is it raining?" Bryce whines.

I did see it in the forecast, but it was supposed to be this evening, not now. "Come over here, we'll stay under the tree until it passes. There are blue skies right behind it."

I drag her over to the part of the river that's canopied under a large tree, then I tie our rafts together using our life vests and grab on to a tree branch.

"It's making it cold." She covers her arms, and I see little goose bumps exploding all over them. I also see her nipples poking through the thin fabric, but I try not to think of that.

"You're welcome to hop in my raft if you'd like." I wink, but she doesn't take the bait because she never does.

The rain only makes the rocks slipperier, which causes my footing to slide.

"Should we just make a go of it?" I ask.

She looks at the rain. A family sails past us with their mouths wide open, pointed at the sky, embracing the rain.

"Well, that makes me feel like a wimp," she says.

"It's up to you."

"Okay, let's just go. I'm soaked anyway, who cares."

I let go of the tree branch and use my feet under the raft to get us moving. Now that we're attached, she can stay right with me. I free us from the shelter, and the rain accosts us, pelting our skin and feeling a little like tiny pinpricks. When my raft stops on a rock, Bryce's raft tips, causing her to slide off hers onto mine.

Suddenly she's halfway on top of me and half in the water. Our eyes lock, and the small amount of space between us feels filled with sexual tension—at least for me. Her in a bikini. Her hands on me, slippery from the sunscreen.

We stare at one another for a moment before she inches up on her arms. "I'm sorry, I don't know…" Her hands slip again, and she falls more on top of me, her breasts crushing against my chest.

I grab her to keep her steady, but I'm distracted by her weight on mine, the smoothness of her body against the hardness of mine. I pull her forward, then release her so she's completely over me. Before I know what I'm doing, my hand runs along her hair, my fingers wrap around the back of her neck, and I'm bringing her face to mine.

Our lips meet, and I know I should stop it because I'll regret it—it won't be enough. I want so much more from her than this. I want her like I had her two years ago. I push that out of my head and enjoy the moment as she takes the initiative and slides her tongue into my mouth.

I groan, and my hand slides down her side, grabbing her plump ass and grinding her along my now hardening length. She deepens the kiss, our tongues battling for dominance while her hips circle along my cock. My hand glides up her body and I'm just about to touch the bottom of her breast, to lift the fabric of her bikini and hold the weight of her tit in my hand, but a kid screams farther up the river, dragging us out of the haze we're in.

She strips her lips off mine, and we stare at one another for a second.

I remove my hands from her, and she scrambles to free herself, falling into the water before grabbing her raft again. We don't say anything as I dislodge myself from the big rock, hoping it didn't tear a hole in my raft.

We travel the rest of the way in silence, me navigating the water to reach the end of our designated tubing tour. I step off my raft to bring it in and help her with hers.

"We can't do that again," she whispers, since our friends are on the hill, waiting for us by the bus that will drive us back to the parking lot where we started.

"I know," I answer.

I walk up the hill, acting as if I don't care, but in reality, I'm wondering what an enemies-with-benefits situation would look like. Just to get her out of my system.

But that's probably a terrible idea because I'm not sure Bryce Burns will ever be out of my system.

CHAPTER 15

BRYCE

A few days later, I walk up to my apartment building to find a man standing there with a suitcase. That man is my father.

"Dad?"

"Bryce," he says in a cheerful voice as if I haven't been dodging his and Mom's calls.

"What are you doing here?" I unlock the outside apartment door because I'm not going to have this conversation with him on the street.

"I got tickets to the Grizzlies. We haven't caught a game together in a long time. Figured it was time." He hauls his suitcase up the stairs beside me.

"I can get us tickets. Cooper is the quarterback, plus I work at *Sportsverse* now."

"Your mom and I are so proud of you. We've subscribed and read every article you've written. Your mom is clipping them out."

I open my apartment door and hold it for him to walk in first. "Dad…"

He holds up his hand. "Listen, we don't have to talk about it now. How about we go to the game, have a nice steak dinner, and then tomorrow morning we have breakfast and talk logistics? Let's just enjoy today."

My shoulders sag. Game days with my dad were always my favorite. He'd pick me up from Mom's, and we'd either watch a local game or he'd fly me to a new stadium. It was what happened after the steak dinners that I didn't care for.

"I can't even get us into a good place this last minute. I might have to get Coop to call in a favor."

"We can have pizza if you'd like. I don't care." He sits on the couch, looking over the apartment. Not judging though—my dad doesn't judge anyone, not even himself, even when he should.

"Steak is the tradition. Let me see what I can do."

I sit down and look up some restaurants on my phone, trying to find a reservation. The universe must be on my side because I scored a table for two tonight after the game. I hurry and book it.

At least he won't talk to me in public about the fact that he and Mom are reconciling. It'd be most kids' dream, but not mine. I saw too many things I can't unsee now.

"So, tell me about your new job." My dad leans back, stretching his arm out across the back of the couch.

I tell him about Shelly giving birth and not knowing she was pregnant and how my assignment with the Grizzlies is only temporary. I'll probably have to go to another team that isn't a national team when she returns from maternity leave, but I'm trying to do everything right so I'll be offered the next opportunity that arises.

"I feel like you've been a little nicer in your articles. Especially to Cavanaugh. Not that he's done a lot to criticize this year."

"Mr. Osterman, our editor, says he hired me for my tough reporting, but then he kind of suggested I play nice when he gave me the position. Shelly is a huge fan of Cavanaugh. Promised him one-on-ones and stuff before she had the baby. I just don't want to make waves."

"That's not the Bryce Burns I know."

I shrug. "Sometimes I have to play by the rules."

He sits up and rests his elbows on his knees. "No, you don't. You report how you see fit. *Sportsverse* is lucky to have you, and if they don't see that, then they're blind."

"You're my dad. You have to say that."

He waves me off. "I told your mom I thought you and Cavanaugh were having some kind of relationship, the way you were complimenting him the other day."

My face screws up and then heats when I remember our kiss on the raft. "Absolutely not."

"I'm kidding, Bryce. Relax." He stares at me for a long time as if he's trying to read my mind.

I stand. "Do you want a drink? I don't have a ton. Water, a few cans of diet soda…"

"Water is fine." My head is buried in the fridge when he brings up the elephant in the room. "Your mom is good. Just had her checkup, and she's still in remission."

He doesn't see me take a deep, relieved breath. "That's good."

"I figured you'd want to know."

I straighten and close the fridge door, bringing him his water. "Of course I do."

Awkwardness paints the room until he speaks again.

"Well, why don't you give me a tour of the city?" he asks.

"Let me grab my coat," I say and disappear to my bedroom, where I send a text to Ellery.

Me: My dad is here. He surprised me.

The three dots appear right away.

Miles: That sounds like it's a bad thing.

I rear back and inspect my phone. Sure enough, I texted the wrong person.

Me: Sorry, that was for Elle.

Miles: I figured.

We don't say anything else, and now I've given him a little kernel into my upbringing. He's probably thinking, "Of course she walked out on me two years ago—she's got daddy issues." Which isn't wrong, but I didn't want him to know that.

I decide not to send the text to Elle, but rather just enjoy the day with my dad. She couldn't go to the game today anyway because she's pulling a double as a favor to someone.

My dad and I visit all the tourist spots—the Willis Tower, Navy Pier, Grant Park. We walk the lakefront and museum campus, talking about everything except the one thing we should. We talk about different players and who will do well this year and why. Upcoming trades we think will happen and the draft prospects. I'm the son my dad never had. Who knows, maybe a son would've understood what he did better than I can.

All I can do is see the hurt in my mom's eyes for years after he left her. The hard work she did to pull herself out of her despair, only for him to reappear years later. I love my dad, but I don't trust him with her.

When it gets closer to game time, we head to the stadium. Being surrounded by tens of thousands of people will make it a lot easier to pretend nothing is lying under the surface.

The Grizzlies won, and as much as I don't want to admit it, I had a lot of fun with my dad. It was like old times. He'd even lean in and explain to me why they're running this and that play as if I don't know.

I had trouble keeping my attention off Miles when he was on the field. The kiss we shared while tubing kept replaying in my head, and my skin would prickle. I swear at one point, he took off his helmet and looked up at where I would usually sit with Elle. Was it disappointment I saw on his face? I don't know, because I'm not sure what he wants from me. He's not a one-night stand kind of guy, so I don't think he wants a repeat of what we've already done. If that was the case, we'd probably have done it already at some point.

"I can't wait for my ribeye. Let's go." My dad claps his hands together and rubs them when we leave the stadium. Then his phone rings, and he excuses himself and walks away to take the call.

I assume it's my mom. It better be my mom.

I use the time to catch up on my emails and see that Shelly has sent me a screenshot she found on social media, showing Miles and me river tubing. What the hell? The person didn't tag us, they didn't even identify me, only Miles, saying how they took the picture but didn't want to interrupt us.

I have no idea how she found it since Miles wasn't tagged, but it's clear she's not happy about it.

• • •

I'm not sure what this is about, but I want to remind you that you're not to sleep with players. We can discuss this in our next meeting.

Her attitude is unwarranted since it's not like the picture shows anything besides the two of us floating side by side. It certainly doesn't show how my raft tipped me into him and that kiss we shared. Or how it warmed me from head to toe when his hands slid under the edge of my swimsuit and gripped my ass, running his hard length right between my thighs.

This picture is just us before any of that happened. There's nothing here that would even indicate that we're together.

Not wanting to deal with this right now, I close the email.

"I always loved it when your cheeks got red from the cold." My dad shows me his phone. "I ordered the Uber."

No need to tell my dad that my cheeks are red from heat, not the cold.

"Perfect," I say.

We wait on the curb, looking for the red sedan that's picking us up.

"Mom said we were on television. It was brief, but they scanned the crowd. She said you looked happy. We were laughing, I guess."

"Oh really?"

"She sounded jealous. Bryce, I really think—"

"We said we'd talk about it tomorrow."

He nods. "Yeah, we did." He points at the street. "There's the car."

I'm still getting used to Chicago traffic, but I'm relieved when we get there, and I step onto the curb. The sooner dinner is over, the sooner we go to bed. And if I can dodge the conversation tomorrow morning, he'll be on his way back home, and we can go back to ignoring one another until I feel up to dealing with him.

The restaurant is quiet and dim when we enter, the fancy tables shoved side by side, trying to squeeze in as many people as they can as though we're cattle at the trough.

The hostess smiles as we approach.

"Reservation for two under Burns," I say while my dad checks our coats.

She looks over her electronic device, her finger sliding down the screen, and frowns. "I don't have that one here."

I pull up my text messages to show her, but she takes the people next in line, showing them to their table.

"What's the matter?" my dad asks.

"She says she doesn't have our reservation, but I have the text confirmation right here." I hold up my phone, and he glances at it.

"Then there shouldn't be a problem."

The hostess returns and I show her the screen. Her eyes scan it, and she makes a noise that says something is wrong. "You reserved at our other location. We're the Gold Coast. You reserved at the one in Rosemont. See the addresses?" She points, and sure enough, one says Chicago, and the other one says Rosemont. "That's why when you booked today there was an opening. We're usually booked out at least two to three weeks at this location."

She's polite and nice, but I turn to my dad with a frown because we're screwed. "Sorry, Dad."

He swings his arm around my shoulders, then thanks the hostess. "Guess pizza is the new tradition."

That's one thing about my dad that's great. He's always easygoing, never makes me feel less than or like it's a big deal when I mess up. Of course, he wasn't much of a parent when I was growing up, so maybe it's just that he's never really filled the authoritarian role in my life.

He heads to the coat check to get our jackets back while I

cancel the reservation at the other location. The circular doors rotate, and a scent so familiar surrounds me that I feel him before I look up to see him standing inside the restaurant, staring at me.

"Bryce," Miles says.

"Do you have a tracker on me or something?" I shouldn't have blurted that out, but every time I'm in distress, this man seems to find me.

He chuckles and scans the area, probably looking for my date. He's let his hair grow a little since the summer, and it's slightly longer. The ends still look damp from his shower. He doesn't have a suit jacket on, but his shirt and slacks fit him perfectly.

"Are you eating here?" he asks, ignoring my remark.

In my peripheral vision, I catch my dad talking to the coat check woman. "No. We were going to, but I made the reservation at the other location by accident." Embarrassment causes me to shift in place, and my attention turns to my dad.

"Oh, well..." He follows my line of sight. "Is that your date?"

I laugh. "My dad."

Miles nods. "Well, in that case."

He walks by me, sliding his body between the wall and me. Every inch of skin feels like a warm blanket on a cold night. He walks over to the hostess, lowering his voice. She looks up at us, smiles, and grabs three menus.

Then Miles comes back over to me, where my dad is holding my coat out to me. "I'd love it if you two would join me for dinner tonight."

"Miles Cavanaugh?" my dad says excitedly, putting out his hand. "Huge fan."

"Unlike your daughter, huh?" Miles says with good humor and shakes my dad's hand.

"Well, if you know my daughter, you know she tends to keep her real feelings bottled up."

Miles's eyes shift to mine, and I swallow past the dryness in my throat. "Would you like to join me for dinner?"

I look at my dad, and he raises his hands. "Your decision."

What choice do I have? This way my dad gets his steak dinner, and I can guarantee our dinner won't be filled with conversation about his and my mom's upcoming wedding and my refusal to attend.

"Sure. Thanks, Miles."

My dad takes the coats back to the coat check, and Miles leans in close. "I like being your savior, though I'm very aware that you can save yourself. That's why I enjoy it so much though."

I turn my head and he's right there, those delectable lips only millimeters away. Our eyes catch and stare into one another's until my dad clears his throat.

Thank God for interruptions.

CHAPTER 16

MILES

The hostess seats us and runs her hand along my shoulder as she leaves. It doesn't mean anything, but Bryce clocks it and raises her eyebrows at me. I wouldn't mind her being jealous. At least it would show me where her feelings for me stand.

She must feel the same tension I do when we're close. Just a brush of her arm, and my dick twitches.

"Thank you for letting us join you, Miles. It's very nice of you," her dad says.

"I come here occasionally. They're good about respecting my privacy. But after that win, I'm happy to have some company."

Which is true. Cooper said he was hoping to take Ellery to dinner if she finished at the hospital in time, and Damon probably has some hot date who plastered herself to him the minute he walked out of the locker room. I thought about inviting a few of my defense teammates, but I don't know them that well, and I didn't want to have to feel "on" tonight.

"You seem like a guy who doesn't mind being alone," her dad says.

"I don't, really, Mr. Burns."

"Please, call me Seth. And that says something about a man. Especially a guy of your caliber." He side-eyes Bryce, and she picks up her menu, blocking herself off from our conversation.

"I think people assume professional football players should be all "alpha male" and loud with huge egos who need an entourage surrounding them, but that's not me."

"Damon," Bryce mumbles, and I laugh.

"What, sweetie?" Seth asks his daughter.

"Damon Siska, he's the classic stereotype of a man who needs his ego stroked. He's also one of those men who never seems satisfied with the woman he has."

I can't see Bryce's eyes behind her menu, but her dad's sharp inhale tells me she just shot him with an insult.

Is that where her issues come from? Did her dad cheat on her mom?

"What's everyone going to order?" I ask to change the conversation. The whole reason I didn't invite anyone else was that I didn't want awkward or forced conversation.

"I'm a ribeye guy. How about you?" Seth puts down his menu.

"New York strip for me."

"Oh, that's Bryce's too."

She glares at me over the menu as if we're not allowed to have anything in common.

"Want to share?" I ask.

Her eyes bore into mine.

Seth laughs. "If you want to eat tonight, I wouldn't suggest it. Bryce isn't one of those salad girls."

She coughs, but it sounds as though she's choking on her saliva.

"It wouldn't be the first time we were fighting over something," I say.

Her dad laughs harder. "Yeah, my girl can be a little hard on you in her articles, can't she?"

"That's putting it mildly. If I didn't know better, I'd wonder if maybe she was trying to hide the fact that she likes me."

Bryce's menu slips from her hands and falls to the floor.

"You okay, sweetie?" her dad asks.

"It just slipped."

I reach down to grab it, and so does she. She stares at me for a moment and mouths, "Stop it."

I mouth back, "What?" with an innocent expression on my face.

She tries to convey something with her eyes, something along the lines of "I wish you would die," so I give her my best smile, full-on pearly whites, which makes her grind her teeth like a little teapot guard dog.

We come up from under the table, and her dad looks at us. "Am I missing something?"

"No," we say in unison.

Thankfully, the waitress comes over. Her dad orders a bottle of wine as a celebration.

"Miles doesn't drink," Bryce says.

My eyes drill into hers.

"Sorry, are you in recovery?" he asks.

"No. I do drink on occasion. I'm just not a very big drinker, but I'd love to share a bottle of wine with you, Seth."

"Great. But of course, don't feel pressured to have one."

"It's the empty calories, right, Miles?" Bryce's voice is sweet, as if she's not knocking me for being a health nut. "The reason you don't drink."

"It's more because I get a headache, and I'm a routine kind of guy. My morning workouts suffer when I've had a few drinks." I tilt my head, telling her the ball is in her court if she wants to toss another insult my way.

"I like it when professional athletes work for what they have. Appreciate that their bodies won't last forever. When you're my age, your skin sags, and no matter how hard you try, the middle just keeps getting bigger." He puts his hand on his stomach and smiles.

"Then Miles is your guy." Bryce's eyebrows raise as she sips her water.

The waitress comes over and does the whole taste-testing-the-wine thing with Seth before pouring each of us a glass.

Seth looks around the table and raises his glass. "Here's to the Grizzlies and winning the Big Game this year."

"That I can toast to." I clink my glass with his and Bryce's.

We order our meal, and Seth keeps the conversation going while Bryce looks around the restaurant a lot, only contributing when her dad asks her a direct question.

"Has Bryce told you that she's been to every football stadium in the United States?" She huffs, and her dad shakes his head. "I'm embarrassing her, but every weekend when she was younger, and I had her, we'd go to a game."

"So, you're the reason she loves football?" I bring my wine glass to my mouth and take a sip.

"I like to think so. Am I, sweetie?" He turns his attention to her.

She shrugs. "I suppose so."

I'm missing something here. I can tell by the tone of her voice.

"Forgive Bryce. Her mother and I divorced when she was only four. We shared custody of Bryce, and a couple years ago, Katie fell ill."

"You didn't *share* custody. You only saw me every other weekend and on Wednesdays. And she didn't *fall ill*, she got cancer." She looks at me with zero emotion. Not even a glimmer of sadness.

Seth sighs. "She's right. But her mom is in remission now and we've rekindled—"

"Dad, he doesn't need to know our life story," she cuts him off.

"I'm just explaining."

"To someone who's essentially a stranger."

I raise my eyebrows. "I thought we were friends?" If her dad wasn't here, I'd remind her just how friendly my cock has been with her pussy.

"You know what I mean. I don't ask you about your upbringing."

"You could though. My parents are still married, live in Connecticut, and were college sweethearts."

She gives me a death stare. "Of course they're still married."

Seth puts his hand on hers. "And yours will be soon too." He turns to me. "We're getting remarried this spring on a beach. It's a new beginning for us."

"That's great," I say with a smile. "Congratulations."

"Maybe you can convince my daughter to attend. She—"

"Dad!"

Seth laughs and takes his two fingers and mimes zipping his lips shut, then tossing the key.

Bryce slides out of her chair. "I have to use the bathroom."

She leaves the table, and Seth's shoulders fall, a bit of his good humor leaving his countenance. "I don't know how to make it up to her."

Bryce is right, this is none of my business. Seth doesn't even know the kind of relationship we have—hot and cold and more cold at that. He doesn't know I slept with her or that I want to sleep with her again. It should be her decision to tell me these things when she feels she can trust me. I don't want Seth to keep spitting out personal details of her life when Bryce clearly doesn't want me to know.

"I'm not sure I can help you, but tonight may not be the time to discuss it. Bryce is very closed off and likes to keep her life private." I fail to mention that's the case especially with me.

His hand slaps the table. "You're right. What am I thinking? I'm just so lost, trying to get my family together again. I don't want to cause Katie any stress, but she's better handling Bryce than I ever was."

"When she gets back, we'll just talk about something else."

He nods and finishes his wine before pouring himself another glass.

I'm talking to Seth about Twyla and Chase when Bryce sits down. "So, I sent them a Grizzlies jersey and said my niece or nephew has to wear it because I'm the uncle. Chase mailed it back, cut up in small pieces."

Seth laughs. Even Bryce's lips tip up.

Our steaks come, and Seth wasn't kidding, Bryce eats every morsel, plus all her brussels sprouts.

We're in the middle of dessert, and Bryce is telling us a story about Ellery and the first time she had to deliver a baby as a resident, when a woman approaches the table.

"Seth? Seth Burns, is that you?" the woman says. She's roughly his age, with bleach-blonde hair and a dress that's a little on the short side.

Bryce stiffens in her chair, her attention remaining on her cheesecake.

"Hi," Seth says, dropping his napkin on his chair and standing to embrace the woman.

Bryce moves the cheesecake around, but she's peeking from the corner of her eye.

"Susette, it's been years."

"Were you here seeing the Grizzlies? Always such a foot-ball nut." She slaps him playfully on the shoulder with the back of her hand.

"This is my daughter, Bryce, and this is Mile Cavanaugh from the Grizzlies," Seth introduces us.

I kind of wish he would've maybe just left the table to have this conversation because it's clear how uncomfortable Bryce is.

"Oh really? That's... wait—you're having a meal with

Miles Cavanaugh?" She puts her hand in front of mine, completely ignoring Bryce.

I shake her hand. "Nice to meet you."

She leans down, giving me a clear view of her cleavage, and whispers, "I'd ask you to sign my tits if we weren't in such a fancy restaurant." Her cackle feels like nails scraping the inside of my skull. She nods to Bryce but focuses her attention back on Seth. "How about we go have a nightcap for old time's sake?"

Bryce's fork slips out of her hands and cascades off the table onto the floor.

I pick up the spare one the waitress gave me, in case Bryce was sharing her dessert, and hand it to her. "Here you go."

"Sorry, Susette. I'm getting married in the spring," Seth says.

"Oh."

"Yeah, I've reconciled with my wife. Bryce's mom." He steps aside, drawing attention to his daughter, but Susette just smiles at her and doesn't address her because Bryce's focus is on her cheesecake and that's all.

"Well, good luck with that. If it doesn't work out, call me." She hands him a card.

I've been handed a lot of phone numbers during my time in the league, and if I was him, I'd rip it up or hand it back. I find myself praying he doesn't pocket it because I don't want Bryce to be even more upset. I think I have all the pieces now on who Seth was when he was divorced, and I figure that's why Bryce doesn't ever want to trust a man with her heart.

He kisses Susette on the cheek, and she leaves with a wave to me, continuing to ignore Bryce. Seth sits down, setting the business card on the edge of the table.

"You're not going to put it in your pocket?" Bryce snipes.

"I'll leave it for the busboy to clean up with the table." Seth stares at his daughter, but she never looks up.

I raise my hand for the waitress and signal for the check. She brings it over, and I hand her my credit card.

"Oh no, Miles, I was going to buy you dinner," Seth says.

"Happy to buy you both dinner."

"I'll pay you back," Bryce mumbles.

"Not necessary."

"Excuse me, I'll meet you guys by coat check. I'm going to go to the bathroom." Seth stands and walks out of the room, Bryce's eyes on his back the entire way.

"You can go if you—"

"Why?" Her angry gaze lands on me. "To stop him? I can't control him. If he's going to cheat, he is. He'll just prove me right."

"I just meant—"

She stands and tosses the napkin on her seat. "Just stay out of it, Miles. Stop treating me like some charity case. I'm fine. I'm capable of handling my own issues."

The waitress brings over the check as Bryce storms away. I leave a tip and sign it. So much for a nice dinner.

CHAPTER 17

BRYCE

swear, the worst city to fly out of is Chicago. I've never in my life experienced more delays than when I'm in this airport. I'm stuck here with the entire Grizzlies team. Most of them sit with their headphones in, but Miles is chatting with Damon and Cooper. The three of them are like the Three Musketeers lately.

At one point, Ronnie Michaels decides to sit down next to me. Again, he's taken off his shoes and has his feet propped up on the seat across from him. His socks are funky ones with little beers, grills, and a number one foam finger.

"I like your socks," I say, because they look like something that needs to be commented on.

"Thanks. My kids get them for me every holiday. Ever have something you say you like, and then that's all you get from there on out? It's socks for my kids. These are tailgating." He wiggles his toes.

I nod. "Aw, I see it now."

"I know you're new to town. There's this bar here that you should go to if you like martinis. They've got all different kinds. I've been there so many times and still haven't had them all. Let me look it up."

Miles walks by and stops briefly when Ronnie says "bar," but pretends he's not eavesdropping. I kind of wish he would sit down. I had plans to work on this week's article, but now I'm stuck talking about martinis when I'm not even a fan of them.

Ronnie drones on about some spicy one he loves the most, but how his ex-wife preferred sweeter drinks. That they were always just too different. I nod because I'm not rude—especially to the man allowing me access to his team. Some general managers don't let reporters travel with their team. They don't want us to overhear certain conversations or see what their players are like off the field. They might think that if I see a married player taking another woman up in an elevator, it could change how I see him on the field. It would certainly change my personal opinion of them, but it wouldn't affect my reporting. But other reporters would feel differently. Some are even looking for a juicy story that has nothing to do with the game.

"Look who has his first ad!" Damon stands on a chair, holding up a magazine with a picture of Miles. He has a sports drink in his hand and is dressed in shorts and a T-shirt. It's his first endorsement that came after his big play at the beginning of the season.

The group of men all clap and cheer, but Miles grabs the magazine from Damon and tosses it on a chair, never one to enjoy any extra attention.

"The kid's having a great year." Ronnie smiles at me.

"He is."

"I hope he enjoys the highs since there are so many lows to the profession."

I glance over and see Damon pretending to box with Miles, and Miles is laughing. It's good to see the stress that always lines his beautiful features lift a little.

"I think he likes it here," I say.

Ronnie glances over his shoulder. "Good. We think he's a

great fit. I had to do some selling on him, but it all worked out."

Normally I might not believe Ronnie—a lot of GMs, scouts, and other people within organizations like to take credit for getting players on their teams—but from the hot and cold reception Miles got when he came here last year, I'd say he's telling the truth.

A voice comes across the intercom, announcing that they're ready to start boarding our plane.

Ronnie slips into his shoes and stretches. "About time. Sucks that there won't be any practice today."

It's getting dark outside when we board, so the team has missed their opportunity to practice before tomorrow's game. I'm used to the team falling asleep on the plane, but the players are wired from all the caffeine they drank while waiting. A few play cards, some play video games, some just talk loudly.

Ronnie asks me to sit next to him and talks with me the entire time about his vision of the team, while I try to appear relaxed and as though every little bump in the air isn't causing me extreme anxiety. He discusses who he's looking to draft, which he sternly tells me is just between us. I'm not sure why he's trusting me—I'm a fill-in.

"Shelly will be back by then," I say.

He stares at me for a second. "I'm not sure she will."

My eyebrows draw down. "Why?"

"I'm not sure I want her back, and if Billy Boy won't listen to me, I'll just refuse to let her travel with the team."

My forehead wrinkles. "I thought everyone here loved her?" The pressure I feel to fill her shoes is unbearable.

"Let's just say there were times I think she was doing more than just reporting. She was always flirting with the players, and I don't condone that. I was a player at one point too. I know what goes on in the hotels, and I'm clear with my players about what I expect, because if a reporter's heart gets broken, guess what happens when they write about my players?" He arches an eyebrow.

Ronnie is known for being the "fun guy." The guy who makes the party better, more exciting. The guy who tells stories until you cry from laughter. But right now, he's staring at me so intently I'm afraid he'll see something in my eyes about Miles. My attraction to him, or maybe he knows we've slept together in the past. Oh my god, does he think I'm hard on Miles because I slept with him, and he assumes Miles tossed me aside?

"I can't say for sure, but Shelly always picked one player to focus on every season. This season was going to be Cavanaugh. Last year it was someone else. I plan on talking to Billy Boy when we get closer to her coming back." He lifts his glass. "Don't think you're going anywhere anytime soon."

I raise my glass, and he clinks it as if we're celebrating, when I really feel as though I'm stealing someone's job out from under them. That, coupled with the fact that Ronnie made it abundantly clear I absolutely cannot act on these feelings for Miles, makes me feel more like mourning than celebrating.

———

After the plane lands, we have to wait for a gate to open up before we can deplane, which means we're really late by the time we take the shuttles to the hotel and get our keys. I head to the reception desk to check in since I don't get the VIP treatment like the team does. They have someone from the hotel assigned to them who hands out the keys in the lobby to all the players.

"Bryce Burns, checking in."

The friendly guy smiles, and his fingers fly across the keyboard.

"You guys did an amazing job checking them all in," I tell him and his coworker.

"We knew they were coming. Got a call when they landed. It's mostly just handing keys over since all the billing is the same."

Which isn't the case for me since my billing is to *Sportsverse.* I take out my company credit card and tap it on the edge of the desk, waiting for the guy to pull up my reservation.

His lips twist, and he side-eyes his coworker. "Um... I think there might have been a mix-up."

My stomach drops. "What?"

Those are not the words you want to hear when you've been sitting at an airport all day, you're tired, and it's practically midnight.

"You booked a king," he says.

"Oh, I'll take whatever. Two doubles are fine." I give him my best "work with me" smile.

"Well, that's not the problem, actually. The problem is that someone gave your room away when you didn't show."

"Didn't show? I had it reserved on a credit card," I say.

"We reserve the right to give away your booking if you're a no-show and haven't contacted us about a late check-in." He cringes, knowing this isn't what I want to hear.

I open my mouth to respond, but before I can, there's a voice beside me.

"Is there a problem here?"

I look to my right, and sure enough, it's who I thought. "Nope. All handled. Go to bed."

Miles gives me that expression that says, "I'm not going anywhere."

"I'm sorry, Ms. Burns. I can call our sister hotel for you, but it's about an hour outside the city. I think you'll have trouble finding any vacant rooms anywhere nearby because of the game tomorrow."

"You have nothing? I'll take anything. I'm not picky." I wish Miles would walk away right now. Why is he even down here?

"I'm sorry. Usually, we'd call first to check before we gave the room away. I'm not sure how it happened."

"You'll stay with me," Miles says as if that's that and turns to the guy. "Can I have another key for my room?"

I spin to face him. "Absolutely not. What do you do, just wait around looking for a damsel in distress or something?"

He laughs. "Yeah, I have nothing better to do with my life than save you."

I turn back to the receptionist. "I'm desperate. Please…"

Both guys behind the counter shake their heads.

"Okay." I take my suitcase and walk away, pushing back my tears of frustration. I pull up my Uber app and figure if I can get a little out of the city, I'll be able to find a room somewhere.

A large figure looms over me.

I don't look up but hold up my hand. "No, Miles. I'm good. I'll figure something out."

"You're being ridiculous. Just come to my room. It's a king. I'll put a divider up between us. We're adults."

I bore my eyes into his. "This isn't some cute little mishap like in a rom-com movie. This is real life, and I have to be a professional here, which means I cannot sleep in your hotel room. It's a conflict of interest."

He steps even closer to me, and I step back, glancing around the lobby. "These are extenuating circumstances."

"I'll stay with Cooper," I blurt, not sure why I didn't think about that earlier.

"He's probably already in bed. Come on, Bryce. I promise to keep my hands to myself."

"That's not what I'm worried about. I'm worried about… it's…" I scour the lobby for any eavesdroppers and lean forward. "The rafting thing."

His eyes light up with mischief. "Oh, you're worried *you* won't resist *me*. Valid concern, but I promise not to walk around in a towel or my boxers, except for when I'm in bed."

"Exactly!" I say way too loudly, and the people behind the front desk look over.

He laughs. "Let's go. We can figure out the logistics to avoid turning the other one on once we're in the room."

He walks over to the elevator, and I stay in place. He turns around and stares at me.

I really, really just want a comfortable bed and some sleep. I do not want to have to travel an hour outside the city and then have to make the trek back in here tomorrow morning. It's already so late. Plus, I've managed to avoid sleeping with the man for two years. Surely, I can handle one night.

I walk over to the elevator, and he presses the up arrow button. Thankfully, the doors open right away, and we're able to get to his room without anyone catching us except for the workers downstairs. I wonder if they have to sign some non-disclosure when the team is staying here.

The minute the door opens, and we're both staring at the king-size bed, fear wraps around me like the arms of an octopus. This was a mistake.

"I gotta get to bed, so you change in the bathroom, and I'll change out here." Miles sounds so calm. Maybe he doesn't have the same sexual energy coursing through him that I do.

I grab my overnight bag and shut the bathroom door behind me, completely aware that he's on the other side of the door, stripping down, probably only in his boxers. I reach into my bag to grab my pajamas, and when the coolness of silk touches my hands, I groan. Holy shit, I forgot what I packed. My silk bottoms and tank set.

There's nothing I can do about it now, so I change, brush my teeth, wash my face, and put on my face cream. I crack open the door and announce that I'm coming out.

He laughs. "You can come out."

I tiptoe out of the bathroom, round the corner to the bed, and all breath whooshes out of me.

Miles is propped up on the bed, his chest bare, wearing a pair of glasses, with a book in his hands. He looks up from his book and smiles at me, then motions to the roll of blankets dividing our space on the bed. "See, it's fine."

For a split second, I think maybe we can do this. That is, until his attention shifts back to me, and my skin heats from his gaze roaming up and down my body. I rush over to the bed and slide under the covers.

God, his scent surrounds me now. This is like a torture chamber.

"Miles," I say softly.

"Uh-huh?"

"Thanks."

"Don't thank me. Seeing you in that pajama set was enough of a thank you."

I pick up my pillow and hit him with it.

He laughs and holds up his hands. "You're welcome, okay? You're welcome."

I put the pillow under my head and shut my eyes, but sleep refuses to come with him so close.

Again, I've put myself in an impossible situation because the truth is, I want Miles Cavanaugh probably as badly as he wants to win the championship this year. I can think of nothing else but him.

CHAPTER 18
BRYCE

After tossing and turning for a while, I lie on my back and stare at the ceiling. Miles turned off the light ten minutes ago, but I don't even hear him breathing next to me.

"You okay over there?" he asks, his voice sounding way too close.

"I'm just a little wired, I think."

"Want to count sheep?"

I chuckle. "No, Miles, I don't."

"When I was younger, I had a hard time calming my brain down at bedtime. I'd get out of bed and go downstairs to my parents… my mom tried everything. She had me count sheep, drink warm milk, and try meditation."

"Did it work?"

"No."

"What did?" I ask.

"Reading. Although not if I'm really into the book. Sometimes I read nonfiction at night because of that."

I smile, thankful he can't see me, because the vision in my head of a young Miles falling asleep with a book on his chest is endearing.

"I've read the comments, you know." There's something in his tone I can't pick out, and given the sudden change of subject, I'm not even sure what he's talking about.

"What do you mean?" I turn on my side and tuck my hands under the pillow, staring at his profile in the dark.

"Reading isn't very macho for a football player. I'm supposed to have this whole alpha persona where I bang on my chest and pound beers."

A laugh bubbles up out of me. "Why on Earth do you think that?"

"Because that's what women say. On those pictures people snap of me at the park with a book, they'll say I should be running with my shirt off or lifting weights, picking up women. Don't get me wrong, there are those who say they love it, but it doesn't go with the image of a football player most people have. Like Damon."

"Do you want to be like Damon?"

"Hell no."

My laughter bounces off the walls of the quiet room from how emphatic he is. The bed shifts, and I watch his outline move with ease to the same position I am, facing me.

"In all seriousness, though, I love the guy. He's a loyal friend. Sucks at being a boyfriend, but…"

"One day I think he'll grow up."

"I don't know, he might be Peter Pan."

"And The Den is Neverland?"

"Pretty much."

We both laugh. Our humor lifts the oppressive cloud that's been over us most of the night—or ever since we slept together, to be more accurate.

"Can I ask you a question, and you don't have to tell me?" I ask.

"On or off the record?"

"Off."

"Okay." There's still a hint of trepidation in his voice, but I decide to go ahead and ask anyway, crossing my fingers that I'm not ruining the moment.

"Why the chip on your shoulder?"

"Ahhh…" He grows quiet, but I hear his breathing now. "Are you sure you want to know? It might make you sympathetic and change what you write about me."

"Not a chance. I'm a professional."

Another deep inhale and release of breath. My hands itch to reach over the blankets between our bodies and hold his hand like he did mine on the airplane. This is something big he's trusting me with, I can tell. Especially since I'm a reporter.

"I was the small kid growing up. Didn't hit puberty until my sophomore year of high school maybe. So I already felt like I had something to prove. Junior year, I became the quarterback. A lot of us in the pros played quarterback in high school. But when I got to Michigan, they moved me to wide receiver."

"A great position."

"I loved it. But when I got drafted, I was moved to safety. My first defensive position, and it took me a while to adjust."

I've done my research on him, so I know most of this.

"Most guys are just happy to be drafted, to have the opportunity to go pro," he adds.

"Yeah, I suppose they are. A lot of guys get moved to different positions. Julian Edelman was a quarterback in college but moved to wide receiver when he hit the pros."

"True, but to me, I felt I was never good enough. Maybe because I lack the typical football player mentality. I don't party, I rarely drink, I enjoy reading, clean eating, and working out."

"You do know that football players aren't just manufactured in a plant where they pop out all the same, right? Cooper isn't like Damon. And look at Chase back in San Francisco, so quiet and reserved, while Brady is outgoing and sometimes boisterous. Lee is subdued. Do I need to continue?"

"You make me feel like it's okay to be different, but in the locker room, different isn't always appreciated or well-liked. In high school mostly. What is it about high school that can just fuck you up in the head? I mean, here I am in the pros, and I'm still messed in the head about some bully my freshman year who made fun of how small I was."

My chest pinches when I think of a younger Miles being harassed by some asshole. "I think the coaches were able to switch your positions because you're versatile. I wouldn't think of it as a bad thing at all. And as far as who you were in high school, no one was the best version of themselves back then."

He nods. "I know. I've just always felt different. But I own it now. I have that chip on my shoulder to remind myself to prove to everyone that I'm where I deserve to be. Now I'm afraid if I lose the chip on my shoulder, I'll grow complacent and fail."

I huff. "It's a lot of pressure you're under."

It's not that I didn't already know that, but these conversations with Miles help me really understand what that pressure means for them day-to-day. It's not just while they're on the football field in a televised game. It's something they carry with them everywhere, always.

"We're judged under a microscope every week," he says.

And it's the truth. There are times I feel bad writing articles about them when they might be at their lowest, knowing I'm likely causing the wound to fester, not heal.

"But at the same time," he continues, "we're paid to perform, just like any other job. If you don't, you get fired."

"Most people aren't being tackled or having to tackle people to keep their job."

"We picked it, and we're paid well for it too. Here I am bitching, and that's why I hate telling people about all that shit because, how can I complain? I'm exactly where I dreamed I'd be when I was ten."

I touch him to let him know I hear him loud and clear, but he grabs my hand and interlocks our fingers.

"Miles," I whisper.

"Now you tell me," he whispers back, continuing to hold my hand.

"What?"

"Your parents. Why are you so hard on your dad? Don't most divorced kids dream of their parents reuniting?"

Heat flows up my arm like warm lava down a volcano as he caresses my hand. "It's a long story and you need your sleep." I try to slide my hand out of his, but he grips it harder.

"I'm wide awake now. Plus, it's just a game, right?"

I giggle. "Now it's just a game?"

"Yeah."

Like him, I take my time, because putting words to my feelings about my parents is hard. Not everyone understands.

"Like he said, I was four when they divorced. I have vague memories of how broken my mom was, but over time, she smiled more, played with me more, and just spent more time with me. My dad got me every other weekend and Wednesday, the typical divorced dad schedule back then."

"Was it hard?" He squeezes my hand, running his thumb over my pointer finger in lazy circles. "I have no idea what that must have been like."

"It sucked. My mom got visibly depressed and angry the closer we got to his weekends. She wouldn't talk to him for the first couple of years. She'd pack my stuff, and when his car pulled up, she would open the front door, hug me, and tell me to walk out to him. She never referred to him by name, just *him*."

"And did you even understand it, being so young?"

I'm glad he's asking questions. It's easier than just telling the story from start to finish.

"All I knew is that Daddy didn't love Mommy anymore. I heard her tell my grandma that right after he left. 'He just doesn't love me anymore,' is what she told my grandma. But then when I turned seven, she met someone, Crew. He'd been divorced and had his kids on the weekend I was home with my mom, so I went from weekends with my mom to weekends with her, Crew, and his two kids. They never spent the night, but we did everything with them. Crew always wanted his kids to have more fun with him than they did with their mom, so we did a lot of things like bowling, amusement parks, and stuff. And when my dad found out that was happening, he decided he'd start taking me to football games every one of his weekends."

"I'm sorry." His voice is soothing and full of sympathy.

"Does it sound that bad?"

"Sounds like a 'who can be a more fun parent' competition."

He's right in a way.

"I guess. The football games were great. My dad would get great seats, we'd pig out on the concession food, and we'd always stay in a hotel. He really is the reason I love the game. Always took the time to explain plays to me."

"Did he play?"

I shake my head although he can't see me well. "One year in college is as far as he got. Dropped out after that. As I got older, we'd go to steak dinners after every game where he'd drink, and I'd get a kiddie cocktail that I thought was the coolest thing ever. I felt so special every time we'd go. But then…" I choke up and push back the emotions clogging my throat.

You can get through this. Stop overthinking it, it was so long ago.

"At thirteen, he told me I could rent a movie in the hotel room, and he left me earlier than he usually did."

"You don't have to tell me if you don't want," Miles says

in a calm voice that makes me want to push away the blankets between us and have him hold me.

"The movie sucked, and I got bored, so I went downstairs
to the lobby where he said he was going to be, but he wasn't
there. I walked by the bar, and he was with a woman in a
corner booth. They were side by side, drinking, and he had
his arm around her shoulders. She was tucked into his side. I
didn't know what to do. I froze at first but then scrambled
back to the bank of elevators. He didn't return until three in
the morning, and his shirt was unbuttoned. I pretended to be
asleep. We woke up, and I never told him. He wasn't cheating
on my mom. They were divorced, but… in some weird way, it
felt like he was cheating on me. Cheating me out of what little
time I had with him. Did he just take me on these outings so
he could pick them up at the hotel at night? All of it only
further reinforced why my parents split and the type of man
he was."

"Your mom was with Crew at the time?"

"No, they didn't make it past two years. The problem
was, it was like that from the time I was thirteen to eighteen.
After that, when we went to games, it was usually just the
local games by my college. It was always different women
and…"

"It took away your belief in love?"

I sit up in bed and wipe the tears teetering on the edges of
my eyelids. "No. I just don't want to be in a relationship."

He follows suit, sitting up, and I take the opportunity to
pull my hand away. "It's okay, Bryce. Everyone has hang-
ups."

"He didn't cheat."

"But he was kind of a womanizer."

I look at him. "He was a good father."

"I think seeing your mom upset and that he couldn't settle
in with anyone, preferred random hookups… that's got to
change your perspective on relationships."

The more he's trying to help, the more upset I feel. "Don't try to psychoanalyze me."

He huffs, and now that my eyes are adjusted to the darkness, I see his shoulders have slumped. "I'm just trying to talk to you. Help you."

"Why though? Why are you always trying to help me? Plenty of women out there would kill to be in my position." I can't look away from him, even though I want to out of self-preservation.

"I only want you," he whispers. "I'm sorry if that upsets you, but it's the truth. I haven't gotten you out of my head for two years. I get it, I do. We'd be putting your job in jeopardy, our friendships with other people could suffer if we don't make it, but none of that seems to matter when I'm around you. I only want to help make your troubles disappear. I just want to make you happy."

My tears threaten to spill over, and I close my eyes to compose myself.

"Can I ask you one last question?" he asks.

I want to say no. I want to beg him to stop. I want to run out of this room onto the streets and scream for mercy. "What?"

"Two years ago, after we hooked up, did you walk out on me because you were afraid or because it really meant nothing to you?"

I don't answer for a beat, but I admit weakly, "Because I was afraid."

He nods as though he knew all along, but how could he? "How long do you plan on running from this?"

I throw the blankets off me and stand, feeling restless and unmoored, like a rabid animal backed into a corner. "I'm not running. You already mentioned everything that's against us."

I walk over to my suitcase. I'll bang down Cooper's door at this point. Miles tosses off his blankets and rounds the edge of the bed to face me. All I smell is him, and it causes the space between my legs to ache.

He puts his hand over mine where it's holding the handle of my suitcase. "At some point, those reasons won't hold up. I'm done being on the sidelines, Bryce. I want to play the game, whether I win or lose. I just want to play." I look up at him, meeting his gaze, and he steps closer. "Put me in, Coach."

I shake my head, desperate and afraid. "We're playing with matches."

"I'll take the risk." He wraps his arms around me, pulling me to his bare chest.

I press my palms on his pecs and look up at him. "Miles, I'm afraid."

"Just say when," he says softly.

"What?"

"When I can kiss you."

He searches my eyes for an answer while my fingers glide down along the ridges of his abs. I want to play. I'm done denying myself and living in fear.

"When." It's barely audible, but he hears me.

He bends his head, and his lips land on mine, beginning a brand-new game of "who wants the other one more."

CHAPTER 19

MILES

walk her backward until her ass falls to the mattress. Using her arms, she scoots up the length of the bed, and I don't let our lips part as I climb with her, both of my knees on either side of her body. I'm not letting her go now that I have her again.

Her back falls to the mattress, and I hold my weight over her with one elbow on the side of her head. "Do you have any idea what you do to me? This slinky pajama outfit almost made me go caveman on you."

I slide my hand up the hem of her silk tank, and her back arches when my hand covers her bare breast. My thumb runs over her nipple, and she moans, pushing up and demanding more. My mouth falls back to hers, my tongue sliding between her parted lips, and I groan when she meets me with the same intensity. In our frenzy, we can't get enough of one another. Her fingers grip my long strands and keep me exactly where I am.

"Fuck, I don't know where to start." I tear my lips away, but I'm unable to stay away from tasting every inch of her, so I drag my lips along her neck to the crevice of her breasts.

I pull her silk tank up and off her, exposing her perfect tits.

Her nipples are hard, and I wrap my mouth around one, sucking it into my mouth with force. There's no being gentle right now.

"Jesus, Miles."

It pops out of my mouth, and I look at her wet lips. Who am I kidding? I need more of that mouth.

My knee moves between her closed legs to give me room between them. She widens her thighs more, and I wedge my hips between them, then grind into her. I groan into her mouth when I feel that she's hot and wet and eager for me. Her nails scrape at my back, and I can't get my tongue deep enough in her mouth. To have her body under my hands feels like the first time I held a football, when I knew I found something special, something I loved.

"Fuck." She throws back her head when I grind my steel length between her legs and lick all the way down her neck before taking a tit into my mouth again. She widens her legs further in demand, and I slide one hand between us, through the gap in the leg of her pajama shorts, then run my fingers through her wetness.

"You're killing me. You're so fucking wet," I murmur against her hot skin. She grinds against my hand, and I press my palm down on her clit to get her off.

"Don't move that hand." She takes what she wants from me, arching her hips. "Oh fuck, it feels so good."

She bucks in slow circles, building the pressure with every hit of my palm. I watch as her orgasm rushes through her like a lion chasing a cheetah. It happens so fast that it wedges satisfaction deep in my chest.

"There is nothing better in this world than watching you get off, Bryce, swear to God."

I slide down her body, grabbing the edges of her pajama bottoms as I go, and pull them down her body until they're off. I toss them aside and nudge her thighs further apart, casting kisses up her inner thigh.

"I think I can still taste you if I think hard enough about it." I run my nose just above her pussy, up and down, teasing her, inhaling the scent of her arousal. They should bottle this up and sell it, it's so enticing.

"Please, Miles, please."

I stop teasing and look up at her. Her eyes are shut, and her body is arched with her hands already full of the comforter.

"Are you begging?" There's no hiding the satisfaction from my voice.

Bryce's eyes fly open and meet my gaze in the death stare of all death stares. "What do you want?" Her eyes narrow.

I love it when she's angry, even better when she's angry, naked, and my mouth is between her legs.

"You can't run. Tomorrow morning, no running." I slide out the tip of my tongue and run it gently over her clit.

"Are you seriously holding my orgasm ransom?" She's trying not to pant and doing a piss-poor job of it.

I nod, smiling, wiggling my tongue under my teeth. "It's up to you. I gave you one for free. The rest you have to make a promise for."

She throws her body into the mattress. "Miles!"

"Shh… someone might hear you."

She grinds her teeth. "Fine, no running."

"Glad we understand each other."

"Miles Cavanaugh, if that tongue of yours isn't on my pussy in one second, I'm going to take you down my throat right before you come and then bite it off."

"Fuck, that's evil."

She arches an eyebrow. "Two can play at this game."

"You play by different rules." I bring her legs over my shoulders and run my tongue along her inner thighs, using the tip of my finger to edge her opening.

She moans, and my tongue circles her clit before sucking it into my mouth. I inch my finger slowly into her opening and listen to her breath turn ragged. She moves her hips, trying to get off on me in her own way, but this time, I control her orgasm.

I hold her hips down with my arm, and she wiggles to get free, but I shake my head, flatten my tongue, and run it up and down her folds. Removing my finger, I grab both sides of her ass, burying my face in her. She circles her hips again, and I slow things down a smidge to get her off without the use of my fingers.

"Miles. You're so good. Do not stop. I'll promise anything right now, just do not stop."

I chuckle, and her hands come down, grabbing the back of my head as her hip circles increase, and her grinding gets harder. She pants and says inaudible things until her stomach sinks in, her entire body tenses, and she moans, coming on my face.

"Shit. Shit. Shit. I can't believe how good you are at this."

I lap up everything she gives me then rise up and take off my boxers. My cock has never been this hard in my life. It borders on painful. "I don't have anything on me."

It kills me to say it, knowing that will likely prevent me from fucking this goddess in front of me.

"I have an IUD…"

"Would you believe me if I told you I haven't slept with anyone since I got to Chicago?"

Her eyes widen. "Really?"

I nod. "You?"

"Me either, and I was at the doctor right before I left because I didn't want the hassle of finding a doctor here right away."

"So you're clean?" we ask in unison, and we both nod.

I lie over her, wedging my head in her opening, and she wraps her arms around me as I ask, "Is this okay?"

"More than okay." She smiles, the rare one that very few

people ever get the opportunity to see, and I can't believe I'm on the receiving end.

I groan and tuck my head into her neck. "So wet."

"You're so hard," she moans. "So big."

I push into her fully and allow her to get used to my size before moving again. She pushes at my chest, rolling me over to my back, and I groan when my dick slips out of her.

She hovers over me, grabs the base of my dick, and slides down on me. "I'm an on-top kind of girl." Her hips move forward, taking my length in and out of her.

I grab her tits and tease her nipples with my thumbs, and they harden even further. She rides me slowly, her hands on my chest for balance, and her head falls back while she rocks up and down. I slide my hand between us, teasing her clit, and she moves faster.

She's like a goddess, taking her pleasure, moving up and down my cock. I could watch her like this forever, but she needs to know who's running things here.

Just as her breath labors, and she's seconds away from coming, I roll us over and slide in behind her before pushing myself back inside her. I hammer into her from behind as my hands explore her tits. At this angle, I can kiss her. Our tongues can't go as deep, but damn, I love kissing her as my dick slides into her wetness.

"I like it on the side," I say against her lips.

She chuckles. She's either too tired to try to put me in a different position, or she's calling a truce.

I continue to fuck her hard but decide that I need more of her eyes, so I slip out of her and move over her, rising up on my hands. "I want to see you when I make you come."

She looks annoyed, but she doesn't dodge my eye contact, staring into my eyes as I enter her body over and over again. When I increase my speed, she clings to me, her eyes hot with arousal.

"Perfect. So fucking perfect." Her nails dig into my back. "I'm gonna come."

"That's my girl."

I almost lose control when I see the transparency in her dark eyes, as if a veil has lifted from them. There's so much there. A plea to not hurt her, to not damage her fragile heart. I'd never do that. Not to her, the woman who's perfect for me.

She arches off the mattress, coming on a curse before sinking back down. I pump into her a few more times before I withdraw and grip the base of my cock, then come all over her stomach.

We lie there for a moment, catching our breath, and I slide the sweaty hair away from her forehead and kiss it. "I'll be right back. Remember, no running."

She shakes her head. "I'm pretty sure you'd catch me at the door."

"True. I am used to chasing faster guys than you." I head into the bathroom and grab a washcloth before returning to clean her up. Wiping her stomach, I ask, "How do you feel now?"

"I think I could sleep for a week."

I laugh. "I might stay awake all night to make sure you don't sneak out."

I return to the bathroom to toss the washcloth in the corner of the bathroom, and when I return, she's sprawled naked on the bed, her eyes closed.

Taking away our barrier, I use the blankets to cover her, trying not to disturb her.

Her eyes pop open, and I jolt back. "I'm not asleep yet."

"You scared the crap out of me."

She laughs and settles under the covers. "Next time I'm coming when I'm on top."

I lie down under the blankets, and I'm pleasantly surprised when she slides over and cuddles into my side. "Are you always going to fight for control?"

She rests her chin on my stomach and looks at me. "Probably."

I grin. "I'd expect nothing less."

We talk about our game tomorrow, or today as it were, and she runs her hand up and down my stomach. I can't remember the last time I was this happy. I can only pray that we don't fuck it up.

Right before I'm about to lose the battle with sleep, she turns to me. "We're on the same page, right?"

"What's that?"

"That this stays between us. No one can know we did this."

I sigh and open my eyes. She opens her mouth to say something, but I place my finger over her mouth. "Just don't run. You don't run away from me, and I'll agree to whatever you want."

She smiles, a soft look in her eyes. "I'm not running."

"Then we have a deal."

We lie there, her body getting heavier the deeper she falls asleep, but I stay awake, hoping I'm not making a mistake. I've never wanted anyone like I want Bryce, but she comes with risks—the biggest one being that she'll freak out and make a run for it.

Hell, I come with risks for her. I should've known my love life wouldn't come easy—nothing ever really has. But I fought to be a pro football player, and I'll fight to be Bryce's man just the same.

CHAPTER 20

BRYCE

The Grizzlies ended up winning the game, and Miles had two deflections and a pick-six that he ran back for thirty yards. I guess sleep isn't necessary for him to play well. Maybe sex is.

When I enter my apartment, I slip off my shoes and throw off my coat. Now that the weather is worse, and we've had a snowstorm, I have to go shopping for an actual winter coat. The wind is unbelievable here.

Booting up my laptop, I grab my open bottle of white wine and a glass from the dishwasher and sit on my couch to work on my article. How do I say all the great things Miles did? Will someone see through me? When I showed up at the game, well after they'd arrived for warm-ups, I swear Cooper looked at me funny, but I'm almost certain I can trust Miles. It's the "almost" part that gives me hives.

Everyone who reads my article will probably have seen the game. He'd get MVP if they passed it out.

My fingers are on my keyboard, ready to dig in, when a buzz from downstairs sounds out of my intercom.

I bring my wine with me and press the button. "Hello?"

"Pizza man," a man clearly disguising his voice says.

"I didn't order pizza, wrong place."

"Seriously?" Miles asks.

I laugh. "What's on this pizza?"

"Spinach and garlic. Stuffed."

"Doesn't sound like clean eating to me."

"I made an exception in the interest of spending time with you."

I smile. "My finger is hovering over the button… did you bring any sides?"

"It comes with at least one orgasm. If you're good and eat all your pizza, maybe two."

I press the button before I spit out my wine. I hear his chuckle through the speaker until the door shuts behind him.

Opening my apartment door, I lean on my open door-frame and wait for him. Of course, Miles doesn't complain like Cooper as he rounds the last set of stairs, holding a pizza box. The guy isn't even breathless.

"Good surprise?" he asks.

"I do have an article to write about a certain someone." I sip my wine, and he doesn't stop walking toward me until he's right in front of me. Holding the pizza box, he takes my wine and sips from the glass then gives it back to me.

"I'd prefer something a little tastier," he says.

"Well, I don't have a lot. Tap water?"

He bends down and kisses me, his tongue sliding into my mouth for the briefest second before he pulls away. "That's what I'm here for."

"Just my mouth?" I give him a sassy smile.

He walks into my apartment, and I shut the door behind him. "Among other parts of you." Glancing over his shoulder into the kitchen, he places the box on the stove and opens it.

"I'm offended you're starting with the pizza." I join him in the kitchen. Standing next to him without heels, I feel like a child. He's so much larger than me. "But that pizza looks so good, I'll let you stay."

He bends down and takes my lips again. "I was hoping the pizza would sway you."

I wind my arm around his neck and hold his head to mine to continue our kiss. "I would have let you stay without the pizza."

He opens all my cabinets, apparently looking for plates, and I love that he's making himself at home, though I'd never admit that to him.

"How did you know where I live?" I ask, propping myself on the counter, watching him move around my space. The giddiness welling up inside me is not a good sign.

"I have my ways."

He dishes out the pizza and opens up drawers until he finds the silverware. Coming over to my side, he slides himself between my legs and places one plate next to me and cuts a piece off his slice of deep dish.

"Do I not get pizza?"

He holds the piece of pizza in front of my mouth. "You're first."

I open, and he inserts the fork into my mouth. My lips slide the pizza off the tines while I meet his gaze. "You're teasing me now." I chew and swallow. "It's so good," I say in a half moan, then grab the fork and cut off a piece of pizza before stabbing it with the fork and holding it in front of his mouth. "Your turn."

He opens his mouth and takes the piece. As I slide the fork out of his mouth, I study him.

"You're right. That's really good. I didn't think I'd like the deep dish, but it's growing on me."

Abandoning the pizza, he wraps his arm around my body, and I wrap my arms around his neck. He picks me up off the counter, walks over to the couch, and places me in front of my computer.

"Now you work," he says and disappears back into the kitchen.

"What are you going to do?"

"I'm going to eat, and then I'm going to read."

I glance at the backpack he must have dropped on the floor when he came in. "How long are you staying?"

He chuckles on his way back into the room, holding two plates of pizza. "Already trying to get rid of me, huh? Don't worry, I just brought a change of clothes, so if I run into Damon when I go home, I can say I've already been out in the morning." He hands me a plate and silverware, and I put it next to my computer.

I should probably be annoyed that he assumes he'll be spending the night, but I can't find it in me to say anything since I find myself wanting him to stay.

Grabbing his backpack, he goes to my chair, sprawling his legs out so they hang off the edge of my coffee table. He eats pizza and reads while I try to focus on my article. But it's hard when there's a hunky, intellectual football player I want to fuck only a few feet away.

"Why'd you come if you knew I had to work?" I ask.

He looks over the edge of his book. "Because there's time for fun after work."

Ever since last night, I can't fight my smiles around him. And the more I smile, the more my resolve not to get emotionally involved dies.

We sit in silence for half an hour, and I get one sentence written. He doesn't purposely tempt me, but knowing he's here and seeing him in my peripheral vision is enough for me to lose all concentration. I finally shut my computer, and he looks at me. I'm not sure what look I give him, but he tosses the book on the table and comes over to me. In seconds, his hands are on either side of my face and his lips are on mine.

"You're not done, are you?" he says after he's already ignited the fire in my veins.

"No." His hands fall from my face, and he shifts a few feet

away on the couch. "I can't concentrate. I just want you so much."

His nostrils flare. "Don't say things like that."

I crawl across the couch and place my hand on his shirt. It's threadbare, so I feel his hard nipple underneath. Nuzzling my head into the crook of his neck, I run my nose up and down, inhaling his scent. "We'll just fool around a little, and then I'll write the article."

He doesn't fight me, so I swing my leg over his lap. His gaze slowly moves over my body, and I push out my tits.

"You're impossible to resist."

I grind down on the bulge in his pants. "I can tell."

His hands land on my hips to keep me from moving, but I continue, and he doesn't stop me.

"I know you want to play," I say, my fingers crawling up his chest.

"When you're done. You'll hate me if you're late sending in your article."

I love that he's concerned, but I don't care in this moment. I just want to feel him inside me. The fullness, the stretching, him sliding through my wetness and into my body.

My hands fall between us, and my fingers slide under the elastic waistband of his track pants. "He wants to come out. I know he does."

"Are you talking about my dick like he's a person?"

I bite my lip and nod.

His head rocks back in laughter. "Shit, Bryce."

He raises his hips, and I slide back on his legs, pulling the track pants down to rest under his balls. He takes a deep inhale, then his stomach sinks in. I can't help but love the control I have right now. His reaction to my actions is so hot. It gets me off as much as when he's trying to control me.

Using his shoulders for balance, I stand up on the couch, my feet on either side of his thighs, my pussy even with his face. "Take off my pants."

I stare down at him, and he watches me intently as his hands lift, and he unbuttons my pants and slides down the zipper. He tugs them down, and I help him shimmy them over my ass. I lift one leg at a time until I'm standing in front of him, my sheer purple underwear dead center in front of his face.

His hands grip my ass and pull me toward him. I allow him a deep inhale and a sweet kiss against the lace before I step back. I straddle his lap once more and he groans, feeling the soaked fabric along his hard dick.

"Why don't you slide them over?" I say.

"First things first." He unbuttons my blouse and spreads it open, sliding his hands so it falls off my shoulders. "Matching set."

I nod, biting my lower lip.

He reaches back and unclips my bra, the straps falling down my arms until he glides them the rest of the way. Sitting on him with nothing but sheer fabric between us, my bare breasts available for his feasting, I no longer care about my article. I want this. I am laser-focused on having my way with this hot-as-fuck man in front of me.

He runs his knuckles down the side of my breast and rib cage before sliding them between my legs. Using one finger, he moves the scrap of lace over, and I rise up to settle the tip of him at my opening. Our eyes lock as I sink down on his length.

He groans, and I place my hands on his shoulders, rocking in place. He takes fistfuls of my ass, helping me get as much friction as possible and pushing him so deep I want to scream. Needing to feel even closer to him, I wrap my arms around his neck, and his breath tickles my ear. He nibbles the loose flesh, and his neediness to have me move slower shows when he breaks any distance between our bodies.

"You feel phenomenal," he says, his breathing hitching

when he looks down at where we're joined. "I'll never get enough."

"I hope not. Miles, I'm so close."

He drills his hips up off the couch, and his dick pushes even deeper inside me. I'm struggling to hold back from going right off the edge.

"Just let it go," he says, sweat collecting between our bodies. "Come."

"I don't want this to end. It feels too good." I throw back my head, and he leans forward and bites the skin on my neck down to my collarbone. "But when you mark me…"

"What?" He continues to cover me with love bites.

"I love it. It makes me feel…" I can barely finish my thought, I'm so lost in the lust I have for this man. The unbelievable way he fucks me with everything he's got.

"What does it make you feel?"

Will he ever just let me babble during my orgasms? Probably not. It's Miles.

He uses his finger to turn my head to face him. "Answer the question, Bryce. It makes you feel…"

I stare into those blue eyes and lose all my bearings, my walls crumbling from the feeling in my gut that's been tugging at me, telling me I can trust him, he's not going to hurt me.

"Bryce."

"That I'm yours. Are you happy? You marking me like some alpha caveman makes me feel like you own me, and as embarrassing as that is for a woman like me, I fucking love it."

His head falls against the back cushion of the couch, his laughter mixed with a groan. He thrusts harder up into me. "Baby, don't be embarrassed. I want to belong to you just as much."

My nails dig into his shoulders because my climax is coming like a freight train that doesn't have brakes.

"Tell anyone, and I'll kill you," I shout, as my orgasm takes over my body. I tense, then all my muscles relax at once as bliss fills me up from the inside.

Miles takes my hips, moving me up and down on his dick until his eyes roll back in his head and my name leaves his lips, sounding like a benediction.

It's only been one day, and I'm already addicted to him. Or his dick. Yeah, of course it's his dick. I've never been with anyone else who knows how to use theirs like he does.

CHAPTER 21

MILES

Having a secret relationship isn't easy.

So instead of having dinner at a nice restaurant downtown, we're sneaking into the planetarium on a weeknight.

Damon told me about this place. Said he took a date here on a weekday once, and she gave him head while the stars swirled above them. He said there's usually no one here during the week, so I thought it was safe to tell Bryce I would sit in the third row from the back on the right side, but when I got there, there was a guy sitting with his head leaned back, eyes closed.

I'm not sure if he's relaxing, sleeping, or dead, but to get away from him, I go to the left side of the theater instead. Then I pull out my phone and text Bryce, so she knows I had to change the plan. She's due here in seven minutes. Yes, she wanted us to arrive at odd times, not exactly at seven or seven thirty, but rather 7:27 and 7:34. I understand that she's risking her job, but I also think there is such a thing as taking it too far.

As I wait in my seat, a teenage couple takes a spot at the very back, closest to the wall, by the exit doors. Pretty sure they're not interested in the show. I'm not either. Just being close to Bryce is good enough for me.

The doors open at exactly 7:26, and it has to be her, but I don't look because that would be a dead giveaway. A figure walks down the aisle, and I try to make out whether it's her or not, but I don't think so because they slide in next to the guy who was napping.

I'm not sure what happens, but I hear a yelp from him and a scream from a woman a minute later.

"Oh my god!" the woman says, and it's a voice I'd recognize anywhere. Bryce stands and rushes out of the theater.

"Fuck," I mumble, following her out. Pushing through the doors, I squint at the bright lights of the lobby.

Bryce is pacing, and I step over to approach her when the guy comes out of the theater behind me.

"Bryce?" he asks. I try to keep walking as though I wasn't about to approach Bryce, but the guy sees me. "Miles Cavanaugh?"

Fuck. It's Grant Thorn, the reporter for *Sportsverse*.

I walk toward them even though Bryce's eyes are telling me to leave. Grant swears the Panthers will win the Bowl this year, but I've heard rumblings that their general manager, Mike O'Leary, bribed him for his opinion. Which means he cannot be trusted.

"Hey." I pretend to get my first view of Bryce. "Bryce?"

She's dressed in black leather pants, heels, and a blouse that dips low to show off her cleavage. She looks hot as hell, and I am not okay with the way Grant is drooling from the side of his mouth like a bulldog right now.

"Miles. What are you doing here?" she asks.

I stuff my hands in my pockets. "Just trying to get away from the noise. I like it here, it's quiet." That's not a lie.

"You aren't here together?" Grant asks.

"No, and I'm really sorry for what happened. I'm

supposed to be meeting, um… someone here." Bryce's cheeks heat.

What the hell happened?

"Well, I hope it's your boyfriend you're meeting with the way you greeted me," Grant says with a laugh.

Bryce glances at me, biting her cheek. Now I'm really curious what she did to him. "Yeah, it's casual."

Grant shakes his head. "You kids these days. There's nothing wrong with an actual relationship."

"Different generations, I guess." She smiles.

Grant glances my way. "Well, I'm going back in. I hope your date shows up, Bryce." He walks back toward the doors to the theater.

I go to break the distance between us, but Bryce puts up her hand at her hip. Fucking hell, I hate this, and it's only been like a week and a half of sneaking around at this point.

"What did you do?" I say under my breath.

Her face turns even more red. "I'm going to get fired. He's going to tell everyone at work. Mr. Osterman is going to hear and fire me."

"It can't be that bad."

Her eyes bore into mine. "I put my hand on his dick and asked him if it'd like to come out and play with my mouth."

I press my lips together because I want to laugh, but I'm not going to do that to her when she's so embarrassed.

"Don't." She points at me.

I hold up my hands. "What?"

"Don't laugh. It's not funny. I thought it was you."

"We'll have to do a redo of that." I wink, and she huffs. "Come on, we clearly can't be seen here."

She shakes her head. "You have to go back in."

I look at the doors and back at her. "I'm not going in without you."

"He thinks you're here to see stars. After he leaves, you can leave. Meet me back at my place."

"This is stupid, Bryce. He doesn't care if I stay or if I go."

A couple walks by, and she steps back. I growl with frustration.

"I put my hand between his legs. You can watch one showing of the trip to Mars."

I push my fingers through my hair and pull on the strands. "When is Shelly returning?"

Her eyes widen. "Do you want me off the Grizzlies?"

I tug her over to a corner so we're more hidden. "If I do, it's only so we can be out in the open."

"How can you even think of that? It's only been, like, ten days. How do we know we're going to work out?"

I'm blown away and instinctively step back as if she's going to throw another punch.

"You know what I mean. Don't look at me like that. We don't know if this is worth sacrificing so much." She doesn't look affected at all, like she can take us or leave us.

"How are we going to know if we're sneaking around all the time?"

Her shoulders fall, and she stares at me for a minute as if I'm the unreasonable one. "Well, it doesn't say much that we're already arguing after ten days."

"I just want to be with you."

"Me too, but you should know that Ronnie Michaels told me he's telling Mr. Osterman he doesn't want Shelly back. He thinks she was too flirty with the players."

I think back to our interview, and yeah, she was pretty flirty. I took it as a compliment, but it felt kind of weird for a reporter to be so invested in me.

"So, you might be reporting on the Grizzlies forever?" I ask.

"Maybe not."

"But for the foreseeable future."

She shrugs. "I don't really know, but you have to go in there and watch the show."

I throw back my head when I really want to fall to the floor, kicking and screaming like a toddler. "Fine."

She smiles. "I'll be waiting naked in my bed."

I shift my weight, staying in place. "I don't like this."

"I know, I hate it too, but please." She puts her hands together, prayer-like.

I move to kiss her, seeing no one is in the lobby, and I still have my hood on, but she practically runs away.

"Miles," she says with the disciplinary tone of my third-grade teacher, when I pushed a girl on the playground, and she cut her knee.

I walk to the doors of the theater, and go back to the seat I had before. I can barely see Grant from where I am, the theater is so dark.

My phone vibrates in my pocket, and I take it out.

BB: I'm going to make this up to you.

Me: Yeah, you are.

Then she sends a picture of her in the bathroom at the planetarium, her pants unbuttoned and zipper down and open, revealing a red pair of panties.

BB: Only for you. Bra matches, too. ;)

Me: You're really testing my willpower here.

BB: :P

I watch the show, and when I walk out of the theater, Grant walks out right after me.

"You're not staying for the next show, Miles? Heard that one's even better."

I clear my throat. "Nah. Early practice in the morning."

"Hope you enjoyed the one you saw."

I nod. "It was good."

He smiles. "Tell Bryce I say hello."

"Will do."

He smiles and heads over toward the restroom.

His hands are on the door when I call, "Why did you say that?"

He gives me a look to say, "I'm an old man. I've been around the block and not stupid." But what he actually says is, "You're friends, correct? Cooper Rice too?"

My head rocks back. "Yeah. We're all friends. I'll make sure to tell her, but you'll probably see her before me."

He chuckles. "Doubtful. See you, Miles."

Then he's through the door, and I say a silent wish that he doesn't suspect anything. Bryce would flip out, and I don't want anything bad to happen to her because of our relationship. I just got her, and I'm not ready to lose her.

I take a taxi to her apartment, leaving my hood on the whole time. When I press the buzzer, the door beeps to let me in.

I run up the stairs and push open the apartment door she's left slightly ajar for me. Slipping off my shoes, I undress on the way to her bedroom, and sure enough, I'm rewarded for the time I wasted watching a trip to Mars by Bryce on her bed in a matching set of red panties and bra.

"I like your style," she says, seeing I'm naked except for my boxer briefs. She crawls up to her knees and puts her hand on my dick. "This is the man I've been waiting to see all day."

"Stop having more of a relationship with my dick than me." I use my body to nudge her onto her back again.

"But I like him."

"And he likes you, believe me. He fucking loves you."

She laughs and loosely wraps her arms around my neck. "Fuck me, Miles."

"You don't have to ask me twice."

I end up staying the night again because we can't get enough of one another. I let go of my reservations about sneaking around because she has every right to be worried about her job. I just wish things could be different. Hopefully, one day, they will be.

CHAPTER 22

BRYCE

'm in the box that Ronnie Michaels reserved for all the Kingsmen family members to watch the Kingsmen play the Grizzlies in Chicago. I can't wait to see everyone. I'm enjoying Chicago, but I miss everyone from San Francisco too. After the game, we're all going back to Peeper's Alley, then we'll hang at one of the guys' places. I refuse to call it The Den.

I pop a shrimp in my mouth, standing by the window, admiring the players stretching and getting ready for the coin toss when a screech sounds from behind me.

"Bryce!"

I turn to find Twyla, arms outstretched. She walks in an overexaggerated waddle on her way over to me.

"You're not nearly big enough to waddle," I say, and she laughs, putting her hand over her modest baby bump.

"I'm so excited to see you! Shayna and Violet are on their way. Theo wanted a Grizzlies jersey. Can't wait until Brady sees him in it." She laughs and eyes the veggies and dip. "Oh, I've been craving carrots like crazy."

"Only you would get a craving for a vegetable," I say. "I'll probably want ice cream or some fattening food nonstop."

She sits on a stool at the high counter. "Bryce Burns, are you actually talking about when you get pregnant?" She touches my forehead.

I swat away her hand. "Stop it."

She examines me for a moment. "Is there someone new?"

I stare into Twyla's eyes, which match her brother's. I hate lying to her. Miles and I agreed last night that we weren't going to tell our friends, but we weren't going to put on a facade that we hate one another either.

"No one new," I answer as honestly as I can. In actuality, Miles isn't someone new. I slept with him two years ago, so technically it's not a full-on lie, right?

"I'm still holding on to the hope that you and my brother may become a thing, but I know… you hate him." She picks up a carrot and drenches it in dip. I'm not sure if her craving is for the carrot or the dip at this point.

"Maybe pigs will fly one day."

She laughs and shakes her head. "He's such a sweet guy, and I know he wants someone to share his life with."

I smile, unsure of what to say. I know he's sweet, and I like Miles, but the rest of my life? I'm not so sure about that.

I hear noises coming down the hall, and I'm relieved to see Shayna, Violet, and Theo in the doorway. We all share a smile and I step over to hug Violet, whispering my congratulations in her ear. She told me last week that she had just found out they were expecting, but so far, she's only told Brady and us girls. She wants to reach the end of her first trimester before they tell Theo he's going to be a big brother or announce it publicly.

I ruffle Theo's hair and hug Shayna tightly. I so badly want to tell her about Miles and get her advice. It's not that I'm closer to Shayna, but she was my first friend out of the three of them. I could probably tell Violet too, but Twyla would likely run off, call her mom, and have our wedding planned in a week if I told her.

"You okay?" Shayna asks, drawing back but holding me by my upper arms.

"I just miss you."

She pulls me into her again for an even tighter hug. "We miss you too. So much."

"Did I miss it?" Elle shows up wearing her scrubs, bent over at the doorframe, and heaving for breath.

I laugh as my friends all turn toward her with varying degrees of concern on their faces.

I'd asked Twyla if it was okay if she joined us in the box since I usually watch the games with her down in the stands. The idea of leaving her down there on her own while I was up here didn't sit right.

"Ellery!" Twyla exclaims, similar to the way she screamed my name, and slides off the stool to hug her.

"Hey…" Elle says, and I mouth Twyla to her. "Twyla."

Elle meets so many people that if you don't have a chart in front of you or a name tag on, she'll never remember your name. A hazard of the job, she says, but she's always been that way. I blame it on the fact that her mind is always going a mile a minute and doesn't ever stop to take everything in. Case in point, she has no idea Cooper Rice, heartthrob of the pro football league, wants her.

"I'll introduce you to the gang." Twyla takes her hand and leads her over to the rest of the girls.

After all introductions are over, we open up some bottles of wine and nibble on some food. Elle and Violet are busy talking in the seats outside the booth while Twyla and Theo have yet to leave the food area.

"Kind of weird, Lee playing against Cooper as quarterback," I say.

Shayna laughs. "I'm just happy I got off for this game. I had to do a lot of convincing, and if they need me, they said I better be prepared to go down to the sidelines."

Shayna is a trainer for the team, so the fact that she can

join us up here instead of being down on the field is awesome.

"Oh, and Lee said if they lose, he's blaming it on the fact that I'm not down there with him. So be prepared." She playfully rolls her eyes.

We sit in the seats inside, mostly watching the game on the television. "I appreciate you being up here. More time without the boys," I say.

"Hey, I'm a boy," Theo says.

"That you are, but I meant the big boys." I give Theo a smile.

He jumps off the stool. "I am a big boy." He puts up both his arms and flexes. "Mommy told me that I'm almost as strong as Dad."

Twyla takes Theo over to check out the dessert tray the staff just brought in.

"How is Hannah?" I ask Violet, who's glancing over her shoulder to make sure Theo's behaving himself.

"She's really good. I think she might be in a R-E-L-A-T-I-O-N-S-H-I-P, but she's keeping it hush-hush." She spells out the word relationship so Theo won't understand, I assume, and then returns to watching the game, which gives me the opportunity to confide in Shayna and get her thoughts if I so choose.

But I don't know. I look around to see if anyone is paying us any attention.

Shayna elbows me. "So, what am I missing?"

"What? Nothing."

"Then why are you looking around everywhere like someone might hear us?"

I blow out a breath and look at the screen. Lee has the ball. Miles is at safety. My man's job is to stop the ball, and Shayna's man's job is to get it to Brady. He releases the ball and Miles follows the wide receiver's hips just like he should and gets in front of it to deflect the ball. The cornerback catches it in the air and runs, gaining Chicago fifteen yards in our direction.

"Shit, I'm going to have to make it up to him tonight," Shayna says.

I want to cheer on my man, but I remain quiet.

"He's had a great year, hasn't he?" she says about Miles.

"He has."

"And you have no criticism? You're just agreeing that he's a great player?" Her eyebrows shoot up to her hairline, and I blow out a breath. Then she stills. "Oh. My. God."

I cover her mouth with my hand, checking that everyone else is distracted.

She moves her head away. "We're going to get a souvenir. Be right back." Shayna stands and grabs my hand, yanking me out of the suite.

"I want—" Twyla stops talking because we're already out the door.

Once we're a good distance away, in a corner of the hallway where no one is, Shayna whips me around. "Spill it."

I shake my head. "There's nothing to talk about."

"You had sex with him?"

"Um…"

"Holy crap. You and Miles. Do you like him? He's not a guy who just wants a girl to fuck around with. He wants a girlfriend. A wife."

I rub my temples from her hammering all this information my way that I'm already aware of. "I know. It hasn't been that long, but as much as I hate to admit it, I like him. A lot."

She lets loose an excited scream, and her feet pop up and down one at a time as she claps. You'd think I was her child who just took their first step she's so excited.

I cover her mouth again. "Do not scream." She bites me, and I retract my hand. "That hurt."

"It was supposed to." Her hands land on my shoulders, and she yanks me into her again for another hug. "I'm so happy for you. And he's already one of us. Such an easy adjustment."

"Stop pushing me down the aisle."

She studies me for a second and laughs. "Oh, you've fallen. I can see it."

"What's with all the secrecy?"

I jump back and spin around, happy to see Elle. I bring my hand to cover my racing heart. "I was worried you were Twyla."

"Because you're fucking her brother?" She crosses her arms.

My mouth drops open. "How do you know?"

"I'm not stupid. Suddenly you're busy every night and have no time for Coop or me. Classic boyfriend behavior. And since Shayna here is as excited as if you said you were dating Chris Hemsworth, I put two and two together. When were you going to tell me?" There's an edge of hurt in her voice that makes me feel guilty.

I sigh. "I didn't want anyone to know, but Shayna guessed, just like you. Apparently, I suck at keeping this quiet. And if my boss or Ronnie Michaels find out, I'm fired."

Elle sets her gaze on me. "Is that the only reason for it being a secret?"

"Why else would it be?"

"I just want to make sure. Sometimes—"

"It is. I promise."

"Good, so when Shelly returns and you're back to the Tundra, we can all celebrate publicly that you're in a relationship." Elle is testing me, and Shayna watches to see my reaction just the same.

I smack on a smile. "Of course."

They don't need to know that Shelly might never come back and I might be the permanent person for the Grizzlies. Which means deciding between my career and a man. I never thought it would be this hard.

"Perfect." Elle slaps on a smile but still looks as though maybe she doesn't believe me.

The three of us go back to the suite, and Twyla looks at my empty hands.

"They were closed, so weird," I say.

She shrugs. "Good thing Theo got his early then."

We watch the rest of the game, and the Grizzlies end up beating the Kingsmen by one. It was crazy and intense, and Miles played phenomenally. He's on his way to more endorsements and interview spots if he keeps this up. If they make it to the Bowl and he plays like this, he'll get the MVP for sure.

After the game, we tell the boys we'll meet them at Peeper's Alley. When we get to the bar, Ruby has saved the back room for us, but her bar top is packed full of the usual men with beer guts and mugs of beer that might be superglued to their dominant hands. I'm not sure the mugs are ever placed on the bar unless it's to tell Ruby they need a refill.

"Seltzer," Shayna orders.

I can't get over there fast enough before Ruby says, "Order a real drink, sweetie. We don't do girly seltzers here."

Shayna looks at me and Elle.

"Seriously, Rubes, you have to get them," I say.

"This is my bar, and I don't have to do anything."

My phone vibrates in my back pocket, so I miss the rest of the conversation as I pull it out and read the text.

MC: Meet me at my place. Top floor. We're
pulling up now. Make an excuse.

How the hell does he think I can make an excuse to leave?

Then an idea comes to mind, and I look at the group. "I

have to take a call from my boss about tonight's game. I'll be right back."

Elle rolls her eyes as if she knows I'm full of shit, but everyone else says okay. Shayna went outside to meet Lee because she fears he's upset because she didn't work the game and they lost.

I take my opportunity to sneak up the back way to the third floor. Damon is so loud when they get out of the Uber that I can hear him coming, so I double-time up the stairs. He might be going to his floor first, and I can't chance him catching me.

I'm heading to the second set of stairs when a voice sounds behind me. "Hey, where do you think you're going?"

I turn around to see Miles. His smile is contagious, and he picks me up in a firefighter's hold, carrying me up the next two floors to his apartment.

"Why am I here?" I ask when he sets me down. "Our friends, your sister is downstairs."

"I needed a few minutes alone with you."

His lips meet mine as he inserts his key into the lock. He opens the door and I fall in as the door gives way. He catches me and lifts me, so I wrap my legs around him.

"I played one of the best games of my life and now I want to have the best sex of my life."

"We can't, we're due downstairs." I strip my lips from him, purposely dodging any more advances.

He lowers my feet to the floor. "I bet I can get you to. I'm surprisingly persuasive."

I shake my head. "Of that, I have no doubt."

"And as you know, I'm surprisingly good in bed. I'm surprisingly good with my tongue, my mouth, and my dick. Even my fingers." He scatters kisses across my neck and up my jawline until he reaches my ear. "Put me in, Coach."

I close my eyes for a moment, urging myself to have some willpower, but who am I kidding?

"When," I say.

He hauls me over his shoulder again, taking me to his bedroom.

I'm in so much trouble. I can't even deny him for just a few hours before everyone disperses and we could sneak out.

CHAPTER 23

MILES

My pants are around my ankles, Bryce is stripped from the waist down, but her heels are still on. I've never been one who craved sex after a great game, but the second I stepped foot off the field, I wanted her. But then, maybe that's no different than if I had a shitty game.

I push into her, and her head falls back to the wall, knocking lightly.

"You okay?" I ask.

"Don't stop."

Her dark eyes overflow with arousal and need. Using my hands, I bring her up and down on my cock, using the wall as leverage.

"I love being inside you," I say, struggling to get the words out as my dick grows harder and my balls tighten, preparing to come. I push it back because no way I'll ever come before her.

Her nails run down the back of my head, through my hair, scratching my scalp. God, she's gorgeous, but I'll never get enough of being inside her.

She comes on my name, and nothing has ever sounded better.

My orgasm rushes through me, and I pump into her, unable to hold off. The adrenaline of the win and having her here is too much for me to handle and I empty inside her with a satisfied groan.

Pounding sounds on my condo door.

We both freeze and look at one another.

"Cavanaugh?" Damon's voice sounds through the apartment and he pounds again.

Bryce kicks my ass with the tip of her heel to get me moving.

Fuck. I drop her, and she slips off the heels, grabs her clothes, and goes into my walk-in closet. Right before she shuts the closet door, she gives me a look, telling me to get rid of him ASAP.

As if that wasn't my plan.

I pull up my pants, grab a hat from my dresser so he doesn't see my freshly fucked hair, and make my way through the condo.

He bangs on the door one more time before I open it, then walks right in. "Shit, I need your help."

"What's wrong?"

He stops just inside and looks around, his chin tilting up a bit. "Is there someone here?"

"No." Damn it. My answer came out too quickly.

He squints and inhales as if he's a canine. Of course, the guy could probably pick up the scent of sex from Canada.

"Bullshit." He looks me over, and I hold up my hands.

"Why are you here?" I ask.

"I need to borrow a shirt." He walks right into my bedroom.

"You have plenty of shirts and mine aren't exactly your style." Damon has clubbing clothes that I would never have in my closet.

"I need a button-down. Everyone looks good down there,

and my housekeeper and laundry lady called in sick all week."

He heads right to my closet and the only thing that might save us is it's a walk-in closet and Bryce is petite. But I'm doubtful we'll pull this off. I glance down to where I just had Bryce on the wall and spot a drop of cum on the floor.

Fuck.

I walk to the bathroom, grab a towel, and toss it on the spot before he turns around.

When he turns around, he takes in the towel. "Not like you to be sloppy."

I ignore his comment and work to get him out of here. "I have some shirts in my front closet that just came back from the cleaners. You can have one of those."

His hands are on the closet door handle, but he turns to look at me over his shoulder.

Take the bait, Damon.

"Cool." He circles back around and looks at the towel again. "Are you sure there's not someone here?"

"We just got home. Who would be here already?" I open my hallway closet and let him look through all the shirts.

"I dunno. You're never home anymore. I came by twice this week."

"What time?" I lean my shoulder on the wall, trying not to act as though my heart is racing.

"It was later than you're usually out. I wanted to talk to you about this woman." He grabs a shirt from the hanger and strips off his T-shirt before putting on my shirt.

"What woman?" I'm quick to change the subject to anything but where I might have been.

"I had this woman over two weeks ago. She was all flirtatious at the club, all over me, but when we got here, she said her stomach hurt. I offered to call her an Uber to take her home because I'm nothing if not a gentleman, but she asked if she could stay the night."

"Weird."

"Right? And I don't usually do overnights."

"You did with that girl from the rooftop before the season started."

He looks away for a moment as though he's remembering her. Could Damon Siska have been bitten by the "let's fuck a second time" bug?

"Well, until she was embarrassed by what we did. Anyway, we ended up watching a movie and stuff. She tells me how her boyfriend hits her and how she's been trying to hide out from him. She figured going home with me, he'd never find her and if he did, I could protect her."

My eyebrows raise. "Shit."

"Yeah, I know."

"So did anything happen?"

"No. I told her to call the police, go to a shelter. I gave her, like, five hundred dollars and said I'd do whatever I could to help her. We could investigate resources in the morning. She slept in the guest room, and when I woke up, she was gone. I tried to find her, but she gave me a fake name. Do you think someone is fucking with me?"

"I don't know."

He buttons up the shirt. "It's just been wreaking havoc in my mind. I told her I'd help her, she went to all that trouble just to leave in the morning. At first, I thought I got played for five hundred bucks, but if that's the case, she's one good actor."

"It's hard. You just never know. That's why I'm always telling you to be careful bringing women home. Most times, it's your word against theirs."

It's something I've been conscious of for a long time. I'm a professional athlete. I'm the one who has the reputation to lose, so I'm always cautious about who I sleep with and who I'm willing to bring back to my place. Damon is chancy and this might be his first time being taken advantage of, but it might not be his last. It's not that I think every woman is devious and a liar, but they're out there.

He finishes buttoning up the shirt and smacks me on the chest. "Let's go."

"I'm just gonna change quick," I say.

His eyes float down my body, landing on my crotch. "Cool. See you down there."

I walk him to the door to make sure he actually leaves so I can lock the door behind him.

"Hey, Bryce!" he yells right before he steps out the door, laughing.

But I grab him by the collar of *my* shirt and pull him inside, shutting the door. I release him as I hear the closet door open in my bedroom. "You knew?"

"It was a guess, but I'm glad I was right." He's grinning like a kid on Christmas morning.

Bryce appears in the doorway of my bedroom, shaking her head. "I think all of our friends went into the wrong field of work. They should be in the FBI." She crosses her arms.

"And you're going to keep it to yourself, right?" I ask him.

Damon laughs. "I don't give a shit if you're fucking, but don't let the bosses find out."

"That you don't need to worry about. You just keep it to yourself," I say.

He laughs again because Damon finds most things funny. "Yeah, yeah. But you two better get downstairs before someone else figures it out. You're not exactly stealth like Ethan Hunt." He starts humming the *Mission Impossible* theme song.

"He's right. I'll go down with Damon. That way, people won't suspect anything. You come down in, like, seven minutes."

Here we go again with the whole time thing.

"Seven?" Damon asks.

"An odd number. It's too suspicious if you do five or ten." Bryce walks over to me.

I'd really prefer if she stayed. I wish I could walk down there and tell all of our best friends that we're together.

"Really? He's at your place every night and you're secretly fucking, but you're worried if he shows up in five minutes rather than seven, it will give you away?"

Bryce narrows her eyes at his sarcastic tone. "Close your eyes, Damon."

"You're gonna kiss, aren't you? I feel like I'm six and walking in on my parents again. I shouldn't have said anything. I'll be right outside." He shuts the door behind him.

I take her in my arms. "Stay."

"It's not time yet. We have to be sure before we can ask all of our friends to keep a secret. As it is, Shayna and Ellery have figured it out too." Her forehead falls to my chest.

I rest my finger under her chin and bring it up so her eyes meet mine. "Then let's just tell them all. You know they'll keep the secret."

Indecision swims in her eyes. She's not one hundred percent sure about us yet.

"Or not." I step back, and she reaches out, but I shake my head. "Just go with Damon. I'll be right down."

"I don't know what to do. What if it gets out? I have everything to lose."

Damon pounds on the door. "Are you coming or what? I don't like to be late to a party."

She pleads with me once again, her eyes begging me to give us a little more time. And I'd rather have her than nothing, so I relent once again.

"Okay. Go. I'll be down in exactly seven minutes."

She smiles, rises on her tiptoes, and kisses my lips. "Thanks for the quickie, but after we're done with our friends, I plan on repaying you." Her hand falls between my legs and she grips my dick.

I don't allow her to drop down to her heels, holding her chin as I kiss her again, this time deepening it so she has something to think about while we're down there with our friends and she can't touch me.

I walk her to the door, and Damon's head rotates our way with a bored expression. "Done, lovebirds?"

"Keep your hands to yourself," I tell Damon.

He stuffs them in his pockets. The two of them walk down the stairs and I hate seeing her go. Shutting the door, all I can think is that I don't want what we have to end, but I'm fed up with the secrecy of our relationship.

Seven minutes go by quickly, and I practically run down the steps. I walk into Peeper's Alley and all the guys on the barstools clap when they see me.

Ruby rounds the bar and hands me a water. "On the house," she says with a wink.

They all talk about what a game I had and how I'm saving the Grizzlies this year. One man razzes another for saying I was the wrong pick. After a few minutes, I thank them all and head toward the back room where everyone is.

Bryce stands in the doorway, smiling from ear to ear. She's happy that I'm finally getting the praise I've been looking for. But her opinion is what matters most to me, and she has no idea. I keep walking toward her, but she turns around and heads to the table with our friends before I can get a chance to say anything to her.

"Miles! Finally!" Twyla stands and plasters herself to me. "I've missed you so much."

I hug my little sister tightly, and when we part, I see her baby bump. It's surreal to see my sister with a baby in her belly. "Look at you."

Her vision follows mine, and she rubs her stomach. "I know, right?"

I go around the table and shake my old teammates' hands, then hug their significant others. I sit in the empty seat by

Bryce, and she runs her hand on my leg under the table, but I can't stop jealousy from taking over from my happiness. Lee's arm is around Shayna. Brady keeps kissing Violet, and Twyla is on Chase's lap as they watch Damon and Cooper play darts.

Realization dawns on me. I want what my teammates have, on the field *and* off. I won't be truly happy without it.

CHAPTER 24
BRYCE

Miles and I stop for coffee at the shop down the street from my place. Well, I make him go in first. We pass one another as I walk in and he's leaving. He winks.

"Bryce!" the barista calls right after I get in line.

Odd that there's another Bryce here. It's not the most common name, so I wait to see what she or he looks like, but no one approaches the counter.

The barista brings over another drink a minute later. "Carl!" She picks up the one that's been sitting there, reads it, and calls, "Bryce!"

I walk over on the off chance that Miles ordered mine. "Can I ask what kind of drink that is?"

"Vanilla latte," she says. "Are you Bryce?"

I smile and nod. "I am."

"Aren't you a lucky one then? That was Miles Cavanaugh who bought you that drink, isn't it?"

I freeze, unsure what to say. "Um…"

"It's okay. I don't work for a gossip mag or anything. It's cute." She shrugs.

"Thanks." I sip my coffee and dig a twenty from my wallet before placing it in the tip bin.

She eyes me. I hope she doesn't take it as a bribe—or maybe I hope she does. As long as she doesn't report this to anyone.

On the L train, I text Miles a thank you for my coffee.

MC: You make it difficult for me to do nice things for you.

Me: I appreciate it so much, I thought I would be late for my meeting with Shelly.

MC: Once we're out in the world, you'll see exactly how I'll treat you.

I don't know how to respond because I'm not sure how we'll ever get to the point where we can be seen as a couple. If Ronnie doesn't allow Shelly back and the job with the Grizzlies is mine, how do we tell our bosses? They expressly forbid our relationship. Even Damon mentioned it the minute he found out about us.

My phone vibrates, and I expect it to be Miles, but it's my mom. I haven't talked to my parents since my dad left the morning after the game. We never had our breakfast—I refused after that woman had come by our table the night before. I was still angry and knew I wasn't in the headspace to talk to my dad about the past, so there's a lot of unfinished business still between us. I've been so consumed with Miles, I haven't addressed it. He's made it easier to avoid that part of my life.

I send Mom to voice mail, not needing to be in that headspace when I meet with Shelly. Which I'm starting to dread. If she's not coming back to the Grizzlies, why do I have to go to her house and fill her in once a week? I feel as if I'm playing both sides and I hate it. Plus, it's my column right now, but I swear she has Mr. Osterman wrapped around her finger.

Descending the stairs from the L station onto the Bucktown streets, I finish my coffee right before I head up to her apartment. I'm tossing the cup in the trash when I see a small note scribbled on the bottom of the cup.

I'll be thinking of you all day. ~ M

God, he is so fucking sweet.

I tear off the bottom of the cup and get off as much of the coffee as I can before putting it in my messenger bag. I can't imagine all the sweet things he would do for me if we were out in the open. A large part of me wants to find out because I've never felt this honored or appreciated by anyone.

I think a part of me knew I'd feel this way two years ago, and that's why I ran.

Now I'm invested and I want to spend all my time with him. It makes me wonder if I should have kept that wall up.

I press the buzzer to Shelly's apartment, and she buzzes me up without asking who it is. I come at the same time every week. As much as I hate going, I do love seeing her little guy, Madden. I didn't realize how fast babies change at that age. Every week when I show up, it's like a completely different child is waiting for me.

Her door is propped open when I reach her apartment and she's dressed in jeans and a sweater, her hair done and her makeup flawless. It's like the old Shelly is back.

"Where's Madden?" I ask.

"He's with my parents for the night. Otherwise, I would never look like this." She pours a cup of coffee. "Want some?"

I shake my head. "Just finished one. Can we get started right away? I don't have a lot of time today."

"Oh, okay. Sorry, I look forward to our days because it's some of the only adult conversation I get. What do you have going on today?" She sits on the couch, placing her coffee on the table next to her and crossing her legs on the cushion.

It's none of her business, but I don't say that. "I have a luncheon."

"Well then, let's get right to it. I have some news that doesn't have much to do with *Sportsverse*, but I got this tip from a girl. She thought I was still the writer for the Grizzlies. I guess she was at some bar or something recently and Miles Cavanaugh picked her up."

My heart bobbles in my throat. I mask my reaction as best as I can. Hopefully I sell it. "I'm sorry?"

"I know, right? Everyone says he's such a good guy, Mr. Intelligent, but she says he took her back to The Den and they had sex, like, three times. He refused to wear a condom and—"

"Are you sure she's a credible source? I mean, she wouldn't be the first woman to make up a story about sleeping with a professional athlete."

My heart hammers like a drumline. This cannot be true. No way he did that. He's been with me all the time. I deny my urge to take out the bottom of a cardboard coffee cup and read his message again. But regardless, my heart cracks a little, hearing my worst fear.

"She sent me a picture of herself on his bed."

A crease forms between my eyebrows. "How do you know it's his bed? Is he in the picture?"

Please say no. Please say no.

"Well, that's where you come in. You're friends with him, right?"

"Not really, and I've never been in his bedroom." My tone is on edge. I'm probably giving myself away.

She picks up her laptop, and a few keystrokes later, she turns it in my direction. Sure enough, the blonde has no shirt on, but the picture doesn't show her breasts because it's been censored. But she's lying on his dark maroon sheets and his glasses are next to her on the nightstand, along with his lamp and the book he's been reading lately.

I swallow the lump in my throat and pretend not to want to bolt from her apartment so I can go demand answers. "When did she sleep with him?"

"She didn't give me specifics, just told me it was after a game."

I do some quick calculations in my head because I'm pretty sure I've been with him every night after his home games for weeks. "But it was recently?"

It had to have been, given the book on his nightstand. Regardless though, he told me he hadn't been with anyone since he arrived in Chicago.

Shelly narrows her eyes. "Why all the questions? I swear that place is like a frat house, the way they bring women in and out. I'm sure if we dig enough, we'd find a story about Cooper too." She sips her coffee.

"You'd be wrong." I school my features. "So. It was recently?"

Shelly nods. "I think she said, like, two weeks ago." She shakes her head. "It doesn't matter. The picture is evidence enough if we can prove it's his bedroom."

"It could be staged. There's no proof it was his place. Not like he's in the picture or anything."

Shelly laughs. "For someone who's so hard on him in your articles, you're sure giving him the benefit of the doubt on this."

She's right, I need to tone down the defensiveness in my

voice. "You just hear stories about this all the time. What's this girl's angle anyway? Why'd she come to you?"

She ignores my question. "Oh, here's her other picture that proves she's actually at Miles's place."

"So there is one of him?" No way. Not Miles. He would never sleep with someone and then sleep with me or vice versa.

"No, but she has an angle where you can see a picture of him at graduation with his parents and sister."

She clicks the button, and there's the framed photo on his dresser. Him in his blue graduation gown with his Summa Cum Laude sash. I know I've seen that photo in his apartment before. Bile rises up my throat.

"Oh."

A smug look crosses her face, and she nods like I told you so. "One day someone is going to out them all."

"Can I use your bathroom?"

"Sure. You know where it is. Excuse all the bath toys on the floor."

I stand, my feet wobbling a bit before I can walk steadily. Once inside, I lock the door and stare in the mirror.

Trust yourself, Bryce. You know this is bullshit. Miles isn't that guy, and deep down, you know that.

I pull out my phone and look at the calendar for all the Grizzlies' games. I've been with him after every one. The only time I wasn't with Miles right after was the snowy away game where he was freshly showered and changed when he came over and brought me pizza. But we had just started then, and technically we weren't in a relationship.

God, we're not technically in a relationship now. We've just been fooling around. We haven't had a conversation about being exclusive.

But then why am I this hurt by this? If he was just a fuck buddy to me, I wouldn't want to go over to the stadium and gouge his eyes out with my fingernails.

I close my eyes and take a deep breath. He didn't do this. I believe in him. I push aside all that negative shit with my dad. Miles is not like my dad. One woman is enough for him.

I flush the toilet to pretend and wash my hands. I need to get out of here and find Miles.

Shelly has her laptop on her lap when I return, and she looks up. "You okay? You look sick or something."

I nod. "Yeah, something I ate must not agree with me. I don't have much from this week anyway. Nothing big to talk about. I was just going to write a piece on what the players' days are like when they travel, ask the guys about their favorite restaurants in certain towns and stuff."

"That's a cute idea. A fluff piece." Her insult cuts. It's stuff I wanted to know back when I was just a fan. "Okay, until next week then."

She's way more chipper than usual, almost giddy, and I hate that she's finding some sort of pleasure in Miles bringing a woman back to The Den.

"See you later. Sorry." I grab my stuff and walk to the door, not saying anything as I leave.

Instead of hopping on the L, I grab an Uber and head directly to the field.

He drops me off, and I stand outside the stadium for a moment. Is this the right place to do this? I'm not sure, but I need to catch Miles before that picture gets released. I know I should trust him outright, but I have to see for myself. My confidence has waned on the ride over here. I have to see his face when I bring it up to put myself at ease.

Walking through the hallways, I find the team in the weight room. I ask Coach Iverson if I can have a word with Miles, with the hopes he just thinks I want a few lines for an article.

I wait in the room I've been using as a space to write when I'm here. Miles steps in a few minutes later. His eyes light up at the sight of me. He doesn't look like a man who's hiding anything.

"Hey," he says, then he must realize something is up because he frowns. "What's wrong?"

"I was just at Shelly's and…"

"What?" He approaches me, but I put up my hand.

"I need you to be straight with me."

"Bryce, what's going on?"

"After the hotel room… were you with anyone else?"

His head rocks back as though I slapped him. "Of course not. Why would you ask that?"

"Because a girl sent Shelly a picture of herself naked on your bed."

His lips twist and his face turns so red it looks as if it's going to pop off his head. It was a bad idea to do this here.

CHAPTER 25

MILES

Today started out so fucking great. I bought Bryce a coffee to surprise her without too many people knowing, although I'm fairly sure the barista recognized me. I hate this sneaking around shit.

But then, just as I'm about to enter the gym at the stadium, Coach Iverson calls me into his office.

"What's up?" I walk in and take a seat across from him.

"You know Pavin injured himself last week?"

My gut twists because I cannot believe this is happening. Pavin is the strong safety, and I'm the free safety. What changes are they making now?

I nod.

"We're bringing in Tre Brummer."

"And?"

He leans back in his chair and takes a deep breath. "We're moving you to strong and bringing him up as free."

I sit there with no words for a beat, trying to rein in my emotions. My performance this season has been incredible and now I have to change positions for the new guy? Sacrifice my ability to continue having the year of my life? "Can I ask why?"

"Well, he's new, and honestly, I'm sure you remember how much more muscle you got when you started in the pros. Tre doesn't have that yet. We can't have him down at strong safety."

So I get screwed. Miles gets screwed again.

He raises his hand before I can say anything. "I get that this isn't ideal, but it's only until Pavin is back from his injury. Hopefully he returns before playoffs and you get your position back."

I've spent years developing my ability at free safety. My job is to deflect, to intercept, to stop them from scoring. Strong safety is a hitter, a tackler. That isn't me. Fucking hell.

"I have no choice?"

He shakes his head. "If I saw any other possibility here, I'd do it. And if something bad goes down and Tre can't handle our level, of course we'll be reevaluating. Ronnie is going to look for another safety to maybe trade for. But you know what it's like for a rookie."

I stand. "That's all?"

"Please don't make a thing out of this, Miles." He stares at me like my father would.

"I'm fine. Just get the kid on some kind of fitness program where he bulks up really quick."

"He already started today."

I nod and walk toward the door.

"I have no doubt you're going to succeed in this role too."

I say nothing and leave his office. I head into the weight room, and I swear word has already traveled through the team because they all stare at me.

"What?" I snipe and head over to Damon and Cooper at the bench press.

They both give me the look. The one Lee, Brady, and Chase gave me when I got my trading papers from the Kingsmen. I'd really like to be on the other side of that look one day.

"It's essentially the same. You'll have your chance at some interceptions too," Cooper says.

Tre is across the gym, working with the trainers, and he is small. I understand why the decision was made. I'm just sick of being the one who has to sacrifice.

My trainer calls me over because I'll need more muscle and bulk to play strong safety.

Everyone keeps their distance from me because I'm a big fucking grump the rest of our workout.

At some point, the door opens and Coach Iverson shouts that I'm needed in the interview room. A little alone time with Bryce is about the only thing that could put a smile on my face today. Maybe she got word and knows I'm upset, wants to check in with me and make sure I'm okay.

I drop my weights and leave the room, trying to school my features so I don't give away that I'm going to see my girl.

The room that Bryce has been using is a vacant office with a window, so there's no way we can actually do anything in there, but I just want to be near her. When I open the door, it takes all my willpower not to cross the room and take her in my arms. But she doesn't look as happy to see me as I am her.

"Hey," I say. "What's wrong?"

She swallows. "I was at Shelly's and…"

"What?" I step forward, but she puts her hand out to stop me.

"I need you to be straight with me."

If she doesn't tell me what the hell is wrong soon, I'm gonna lose my shit.

"Bryce, what's going on?"

"After the hotel room… were you with anyone else?"

It feels as if she just gut-punched me. "Of course not. Why would you ask that?"

She looks down and back up. "Because a girl sent Shelly a picture of herself naked on your bed."

Red hot lava flows through my veins. My fists clench, my

body tenses. I want to punch something right now because how could she actually be standing here and asking me this?

"And you think she's telling the truth?"

"No."

"But you ran over here, pulled me out of a workout to ask me about it. This seems more like a conversation for tonight after both of our workdays are done. If the roles were reversed, I would've said you're never gonna believe this, guess what some guy is saying. But you… you believe her."

She throws her hands in the air. "No… but I thought maybe it was before we were really together. I mean, we're not…"

"What, Bryce? What aren't we?" I've felt my tipping point coming for the last week and I'm unable to hold back the hurt that she thinks so little of us.

"We're sneaking around. It hasn't been that long. I don't know how to classify us."

I rock my head back and laugh. "You know what I would've said if you'd asked?"

She says nothing, so I continue.

"I would've said you're my girlfriend. That I can't wait until I can tell the whole fucking world you're mine. That's what I would say. And I sure as shit wouldn't believe some random guy who probably photoshopped himself into a picture when he says he slept with you."

"You can understand why I might have thought—"

"No, I can't!"

Her gaze flies to the window and I lose the rest of my self-control.

"Oh, is someone looking?" I ask. "Maybe I should come back at 3:02. Is that random enough for you?"

"We agreed to be a secret. My job. Your job. We can't put those in jeopardy."

My fists clench at my sides. "I'm starting to think you'll always have an excuse because it gives you one foot out the door. Jesus Christ, do you know how insulted I am that you believe this girl?"

"She was in your bedroom, Miles. She took a picture at an angle that shows a framed photo of you and your family on your graduation day. The book you've been reading was on the dresser next to your glasses. It was your bedroom!"

"I don't know how that's even possible, but that doesn't mean I fucked her. I've only slept with you since that hotel room and I haven't been with one other woman since I stepped foot in Chicago. I told you that. What else do I have to do so you'll believe me? It's only ever been you."

A tear slips down her cheek, but she wipes it angrily. "Stop yelling at me then."

I throw up my hands then put them on my hips. "How did you think I would act when you accused me of fucking around? That I would just be like, 'Hey, I get it, I do. I've given you all these signs that maybe I'm not that into you?' But I haven't. It's just you wanting to keep that wall up between us, so you can always point the finger at someone else. Well, this is on you."

"What?" Her voice is so small that I take a deep breath to get myself under control.

"I'm walking out of here before one of us says something we can't take back. I'll see you tonight at your house, and we'll talk."

"No. Either we talk now or never."

"This really isn't the time to try to demand control of the situation." I step back toward the door, my hand on the doorknob at my back.

"If you can't understand why I was worried and you can't reassure me without yelling, then I don't see this ever working out. You're going to be a professional football player, and I won't always be able to travel with you. I have to trust you."

I laugh. "So, that's it?"

"You decide."

"Why would I? You already did. Goodbye, Bryce." I open the door and walk out, slamming it behind me.

"What the hell is going on, man?" Damon pushes my chest to get me to walk to the locker room instead of the weight room. "Hell, you're lucky I was walking by and told some people you were arguing about an article she wanted to write about you."

I remove my arms from his. "Doesn't matter. We're over."

"Over?" he asks but opens the door to the locker room and shoves me inside. "That can't be true."

"It is. She doesn't trust me. Some girl said she slept with me. Took a picture naked on my bed somehow, so she came here to accuse me of cheating on her. Give me a fucking break. She has so many trust issues and I've tried, but it's over now."

Damon stares at me with his hands on his hips. "I don't think you mean that."

He clicks on the television—probably because he fears people will hear me without our voices being drowned out.

"Claims are being made that Chicago Grizzlies players refer to their four-flat on the Northside as The Den. Two of the players who have lived there initiated relationships with *Sportsverse* reporters in order to get good press. One player involved is a newer member of the team, Miles Cavanaugh, and the reporter? *Sportsverse*'s newest addition, Bryce Burns. More on that when we return."

"Jesus." Damon turns up the volume, but it goes to commercial.

We both grab our phones, and there's a stream of text messages from my friends in San Francisco. I skip over them, going to the internet to see the latest news, including an article written and released today on a famous celebrity gossip blog. The article was written by Shelly Breckles, *former Sportsverse Magazine* writer.

I stand to go back and find Bryce, but Ronnie storms in, shoeless. "What the hell just happened?"

I freeze, and all our attention falls on the television as the story continues after the commercial break.

"And as if sleeping with Bryce Burns wasn't enough, Cavanaugh was seeing other women at the same time. Here's one alleged woman who said Cavanaugh picked her up at a club and brought her home."

In the picture, they circle the framed photo from my graduation as proof that it's my bed. But I don't have that picture in my bedroom. That picture is the only one of myself in my apartment and it sits on a table by the couch.

Damon's jaw is hanging open, staring at the woman sprawled on my bed, although all her private areas are covered in black.

"That's her," he says, pointing at the TV.

"Who?" I ask.

"That's the girl who said her boyfriend hit her. The one I gave five hundred dollars to. How did she get on your bed?"

I close my eyes. Clearly this is a setup and a damn convincing one. And with her unresolved feelings about her dad, this whole thing fits right into the narrative that likely runs through her brain. I've already done so much damage, all the things I said, I can't take them back now.

I throw my head in my hands and close my eyes. Today just ended with a big fuck you.

CHAPTER 26

BRYCE

Mr. Osterman calls me into his office, and I already know what's going to happen, but I'm surprised to see Ronnie Michaels on his couch.

"Please come in, Bryce." Mr. Osterman waves me in.

I shut the door behind me. I'm embarrassed enough to be here, let alone have someone else overhear this conversation.

"Sit." He gestures to the couch with Ronnie on it.

"Mr. Michaels." I put my hand out to Ronnie and he shakes it.

Sitting next to Ronnie, I notice he's slipped off his shoes and has one sock that looks like a pencil and another sock that looks like a piece of paper. He wiggles his toes as though he knows I'm looking.

Mr. Osterman walks over and sits in the chair closer to Ronnie. Probably so they remain a united front. "I'm glad you were able to come in and talk to us."

What choice do I have?

"Of course." I cross my ankles and link my hands together on my lap, conveying my best schoolgirl pose.

"You've heard about Shelly going to the gossip magazine and doing an exposé on The Den?"

"I have."

It's everywhere. All over the news, the internet, and people are believing it, saying Miles Cavanaugh fooled us all as the good guy in the league. It's disgusting how fast they turned on him.

"And as to your involvement in it... my first question is whether you entered into a relationship with Miles Cavanaugh since being employed with *Sportsverse*?"

After I swallow, I nod. "I did."

"And did you feel forced into this relationship?" Ronnie asks. "Did Miles come on to you and did you feel too uncomfortable to say no?"

My face screws up. "What?"

Ronnie's face has no expression.

"No. Not at all," I say.

"When did this relationship start?" Mr. Osterman asks.

"Um... one night at the hotel..." I'm giving way too many specifics. "A little more than a month ago."

"And prior to being employed at *Sportsverse*, were you in a relationship?"

"No." They don't need to know about two years ago.

"And did your involvement with one of the Grizzly players change the way you would have written an article for us?" Mr. Osterman crosses his legs. He's not writing anything down, but I feel as though maybe there's a tape recorder in the room somewhere. Or maybe I'm just paranoid after Shelly.

"No. As you're both aware, Miles is having a great season as safety with the Grizzlies. I understand that I've been hard on him before, but this year, he's given me no reason to write anything but positive things."

"Let's see how he fares now that he's strong safety. Hopefully he can keep up," Ronnie says to Mr. Osterman.

"Excuse me?" My head tilts.

"He didn't tell you? Pavin is out for a few weeks, so

Cavanaugh's stepping in as strong safety and we're putting Tre Brummer on free safety."

"But…" They both glare at me, and I shut my mouth. It's a stupid decision. Taking Miles out of free safety after he's saved his team so many opposing points is straight-up stupidity. "When did he find out?"

"Yesterday morning. Right before all this broke." Ronnie whirls his finger in the air.

My heart sinks into my stomach. He'd just been given that horrible news, then I came to the stadium and accused him of cheating on me.

"Bryce, let's stay on point here. You knew the rules. You're not to become involved with any of the players on the teams you report on."

"And I told you I had a similar rule for my players," Ronnie adds. "Miles knew that as well."

"It's over. We're not even together anymore. Penalize me, but not him." I grab my bag, not wanting to sit here any longer.

"I'm glad you think that because from today forward, you're suspended from your reporting duties on the Chicago Grizzlies," Ronnie says. "Grant Thorn is taking over. Please leave him any of your notes that you feel are valuable."

Grant Thorn. Of course that jackass got it.

"Anything else?" I ask, keeping my chin up and scraping together what little pride I still have left.

"That's all," Ronnie says.

"I'll be in touch as far as *Sportsverse* is concerned. I need to speak with human resources," Mr. Osterman says, dismissing me and not standing to see me out.

Ronnie puts out his hand. "I'm sorry, Bryce, I really enjoyed having you report for us. I wish things could've worked out, but I'm sure you can see the conflict of interest?"

I nod, shaking his hand before putting my bag crossways

over my shoulders. "Thank you. Good luck with the rest of the season."

I walk toward the door, my mind swimming with a million thoughts. Opening the door, I head over to my cubicle and find Grant Thorn already there, opening the drawers of my desk.

"Excuse me, what are you doing?"

He backs up and hits the corner of my cubicle with his back. "I thought you were suspended."

I step forward and he practically slides out of my way. "Just came to leave my notes here for you. What is your problem?"

"Nothing," he says.

I pull my notes from my bag and toss them on the desk. I have nothing personal here because I rarely worked in the office. When I turn, he's still there. "I left my notes there. Have at it."

I start to leave, but he clears his throat. "Anything about the planetarium in here?"

I circle back around, and he holds up the papers with a cocky smirk. I stomp over, grab the papers, and rip them in half, then in half again.

"What are you doing?"

I toss them in the trash can. "You seem to think you're the man. Figure it all out for yourself. I assume you're the one who outed me?"

He laughs. "You guys were so deer in headlights, it was obvious. Shelly baited you yesterday, and she said you were so pale she thought you'd pass out when she showed you the picture. That confirmed it."

My mouth drops open. "You set me up?"

He shakes his head. "I didn't do anything. It was Shelly. You just played into her hands. If she came out, then she's a woman scorned, but having you in a relationship with one of them changed the game."

I don't know what he means by the woman scorned thing, though I intend to find out. But I have more pressing things on my mind at the moment. "So, the girl in Miles's bed…"

He laughs. "Don't ask me, but Shelly's cutthroat. I'll tell you that much."

I step forward. "Are you sure you're a reporter?"

"Why would you ask that?" He seems affronted. Good.

"Most reporters can keep secrets, and you seem to be telling everyone's. First Miles and me, and now all of Shelly's."

"I just wanted you to know." He shrugs. "You came in here thinking you were the best and we should be bowing at your feet. And look what happened. You made a rookie mistake and slept with the subject. I mean, you did pick a good one. Shelly did not, however, which is why she's so bitter and broken. But I wanted to see your face when I told you how it all came about."

I stare long and hard at him. "You're an asshole."

He puts his hand over his heart. "Tell me something I might actually give a shit about."

I inhale a deep breath and compose myself before walking away and pressing the elevator button, but then I think about my suspension and how handcuffed I felt here, expected to write what they wanted me to. As the elevator doors open, I turn in the opposite direction and walk down to Mr. Osterman's office. His secretary yells at me as I barge into his office without knocking.

They're still seated where I left them, and they both look at me.

"Thank you for this opportunity, Mr. Osterman, but I quit." I don't wait for him to respond, walking right back out the door.

I take the elevator down to ground level, hop on a train to my apartment, and pack a bag. Before I run to Miles to try to make things right, I need to handle my own shit so I can be ready for our future.

I order an Uber, and he drives me to the airport. Amazingly, I find a flight leaving in an hour, make it through security, and I'm on the plane before I even have time to think about changing my mind. I land in Idaho and rent a car, then I drive to my mom's house.

I have no idea what I'm going to say, but this has been a long time coming. Miles hasn't tried to call me since our fight yesterday, but he's probably dealing with a lot of fallout too. I just hope by the time I make peace with this, he'll have forgiven me and will take me back. My biggest fear is that I'm too late.

I pull onto the street of the small three-bedroom house I grew up in, situated in the neighborhood that made me who I am. It's been too long since I've come back. After I step out of the car, I pop the trunk, grab my bag, and wheel my suitcase up the driveway to the walkway. The front door opens before I can ring the bell and my mom stands there.

"Bryce?" She says my name as though I'm a mirage.

She looks so healthy I beat myself up for not coming sooner. This is the mom I dreamed would return to my life after all her treatments and I've been avoiding her.

"Mom." Tears stream down my face. I drop my suitcase and walk right into her arms. "I messed up."

CHAPTER 27

MILES

buzz up to Bryce's apartment, but she doesn't answer. I refuse to leave all of this like we did. If we break up, we talk it over. We don't do it in the heat of the moment during an argument when emotions are high.

But once again, she doesn't answer, so I grab a coffee from the corner place and sit to people watch. I could call her, but I want to talk face to face. She hasn't accepted my calls anyway, so my only option is to surprise her at her house.

Cooper and Ellery say they haven't really talked to her. Bryce said she needed time, and they know her well enough to give it to her. Ellery pleaded with me to let it go and let her come to me, but I'm not that kind of guy. I want Bryce, and I'm going to fight for her.

A little girl runs down the street, and her dad chases her, picking her up right before she's about to collide with a trash can. The mom is behind them, wheeling an empty stroller. They walk into the coffee shop and the little girl inspects the space as though it's exciting when it's just a boring old coffee place.

The dad puts his arm around the mom, and he pulls her closer, kissing her temple. They do this dance of him handing off the daughter to the mom while he pays for their order. The dad gives the little girl a cookie, and the mom shakes her head, but she's smiling. The girl's eyes widen into saucers, and she hugs her dad's leg. The mom says something to the dad and they both laugh.

Jealousy gnaws at my insides. That's what I want, and I've wanted it for a long time. I want a family, and I'm not going to be ashamed of that. Bryce and I have to be on the same page though, because I'm already way too invested not to have that with her. If she doesn't have the same desire for a family, for a life together, I need to cut it off because I'll never be able to keep my dreams of the life I want with her at bay.

Leaving the coffee shop, still impatient to talk to her, I go back to her apartment. I press the buzzer again and no one answers. As I'm about to press it again, an elderly woman walks out of the door. I want to slide through it, but the woman eyes me. Fuck it.

I step forward, and she presses her hand on my chest.

"I'll use my cane," she says.

I look down and sure as shit, her hand is clenched around the handle of a cane. "Sorry, I'm looking for the brunette who lives on the third floor. Bryce?"

The woman comes all the way out and the door closes behind her. "You're that player. The football guy." She rests her cane on the building and puts on her hat, then a scarf and mittens. "When you're old, you're always cold."

"Yeah, you don't need to explain yourself," I say.

"But I'm assuming you do. I'm her neighbor, and all I've heard this morning is her buzzer going off. Did you do something stupid?" She picks up her cane.

"Yeah."

"Are you going to do it again?"

I shake my head emphatically. "No."

"Okay, well, I'm a softie, so you're in luck. I'm not letting you into that apartment building, but I'll tell you this—there's been no movement in her apartment since yesterday."

My shoulders slump. She's not staying with Ellery or Cooper. Damon wouldn't put her up without telling me. Where the hell could she be?

"Okay, thanks."

She pats me on the stomach. "Keep up the good work, and if this works, I'd happily take some tickets as a thank you."

I laugh. "If she takes me back, they're all yours."

She smiles and walks down the street but stops when two kids almost run her over. "Who raised you? A stray dog?" she shouts at them.

I watch her go and look up at the apartment. "Where are you, Bryce?" I mumble to myself.

———

I catch the L train back to my place and stop at Peeper's Alley. It's a quiet day, no game for the Colts because it's midweek, so I sit on an empty barstool.

"Water?" Ruby asks.

"Whiskey, two shots."

She studies me for a moment, then grabs the bottle. All the regulars turn like robots to face me. She puts two shot glasses in front of me and pours the whiskey. I move to pick one up, but she puts her hand over it. For the first time, I notice her age spots.

"Before you do this. Are you sure you want to?"

"I just want it to go away." I sound pathetic even to my own ears.

She takes the shot out of my hand, then the other one, and dumps them in the sink.

"What a waste, Rubes!" a man farther down the bar shouts. "I would've drank 'em."

"You've had enough," she warns with her stern voice and

eyes, then turns to me. "Alcohol numbs. It doesn't take it away."

"So if I said I wanted to numb it?"

"Sorry, no take-backs. If you want it to go away, you have to do something to fix it, not wallow here on a barstool. Action." She grabs a water out of the cooler, cracks the top, and slides it across the bar to me. "You drink this and think about what action you can take to win her back. The brunette, right? Bryce?"

"Seriously, how does everyone know? We were so careful." I let my chin tip down and shake my head.

She laughs. "It's all in the eyes. You gave it away, but she did too. I've been working a bar for years. You think I can't see when two people are into each other?"

I sit and drink my water, watching the television. As if I need to be reminded, another talk show is discussing the article written by Shelly Breckles.

"So, did you do it with the girl?" the man closest to me asks.

I scowl at him. "No."

"Yeah, we didn't think so. Now Damon—" the second guy in says, and they all nod.

"Damon what?" Damon asks as he walks in through the back door.

"Would've slept with that girl while you were with Bryce," I inform him because I'd love the fire to be at someone else's feet.

"Bullshit. When I decide I want to, I'll be in a relationship, and I'll be faithful." He smacks me on the shoulder. "I just heard that she's in Idaho."

I straighten in my seat. "What?"

"She's with her mom and dad. She told Ellery that she needed to get away, Coop said."

"From me." My shoulders sag and I gulp more water.

"Action. Action. Action," Ruby repeats.

"What is she going on about?" Damon asks, nodding in her direction.

"She's talking about me taking action."

Damon looks at her. "What kind of action is he supposed to take? He tried to go to her house. She ran out of town."

The word *ran* plays on repeat in my head. Two years ago, she ran from me too. There wasn't anything I could do then, I had no idea why she was running, but this time around, it's different.

I look at Damon, and he squints, clearly trying to understand my look. Then his eyes widen as I stand from the chair. He holds me back with both hands. "No. No fucking way."

"It's the only way. She deserves her job."

"You're delusional. She's just one girl. One of how many possibilities?"

I turn around and laugh. "I really hope one day you understand, because I'd hate for you to never know this feeling."

"What feeling? Heartbroken? Handcuffed?"

Ruby walks around the bar and smacks him on the back of the head. "The love of a woman is a very special thing."

"Yes, Ruby, I know. That's why there's a woman in my bed most nights."

She smacks him again.

"Hey, that's just mean," Damon says.

"You want to see mean, I'll give you mean." She glares at him.

I leave them to it, but as I'm waiting for my Uber, Damon comes out and stands next to me.

"What are you doing?" I ask.

"Going with you."

"Um… no. I don't need you trying to convince me to not do it." The Uber arrives and I slide into the back seat.

Damon gets in right beside me. "I won't. I just want to see what this is like."

The Uber pulls away from the curb. Twenty minutes later, we're outside the stadium. I stand outside and soak it in. I sure am going to miss it here.

"I'm just gonna ask this one more time, are you sure?" He clamps me on the shoulder as I stare at the full-body picture of me on a giant flag outside the stadium, next to flags featuring Cooper and Damon.

I was really making things happen here. But Bryce comes to my mind again. The feeling I get around her is way more powerful and important than when I get a pick-six. Football won't be here forever, but hopefully she will.

"Yeah, I'm sure."

We go up to the front office, and I knock on Ronnie Michaels's open door.

He has his feet up on the corner of his desk as he eats an apple. "Cavanaugh, come in."

I sit in the chair across from him. He opens his mouth to speak, but I quickly interrupt him. "Can I say my piece first?"

He nods and motions for me to continue.

The fact that he hasn't called me into his office at all since the article went out tells me Bryce is going to fall on the sword for this, and that's unfair.

"I know you have an in with Mr. Osterman over at *Sportsverse*. I want Bryce to keep her job, and if she can't, I'm going to make your life a living hell."

CHAPTER 28
BRYCE

'm sitting on my mom's patio, sipping a beer while my dad grills kabobs. They insisted on feeding me after I told them I'd lost my job.

My mom walks past, her hand running through my hair. "We'll fill our bellies. Everything looks better after you eat."

I smile because she's so optimistic. Even during her treatments, while tears welled in my eyes as the doctor told us what we were dealing with, she would squeeze my hand and say, "It's all good. We're good." I felt so weak compared to her.

She set a plate next to my dad at the grill and he wraps his arm around her, kissing the top of her head. She turns around to head back into the kitchen and I see guilt on her face. Because she doesn't want to make this harder on me.

"I'm not gonna stop touching my fiancée just because you're here," my dad says, turning the kabobs over, never looking at me.

"I didn't say anything."

"I'm just sayin'. You need to stop trying to make your mother feel guilty, too."

"Jeez, Dad. I'm so happy I'm home."

He shuts the grill and turns to look at me, tongs in his hand. "I'm glad you're home. There're a lot of things we need to clear up, and I'm sorry about you losing your job. I could've told you at that dinner you were about to fall for that boy."

"Someone's been on the internet." I sip my beer and strip my eyes away from him.

"It's hard to miss." He raises his eyebrows. "You've always done things big, never mediocre."

"You're just full of compliments tonight." I press my hands on the sides of the lounge chair to get up.

"Sit back down." He points at me with the tongs.

My dad rarely ever disciplined me. He never wanted me not to want to go with him, so he might have sternly said something, but this tone isn't one that was ever directed to me. Regardless, I sit.

"It wasn't an insult. You're where you are because you believe in yourself and don't let anyone tell you who you can be. That's an admirable trait. But when things don't go how you want, you like to bury your head in the sand."

I turn away and look at the backyard. Thankfully, they live in southern Idaho, so it's still warmer here even if there's a bit of chill in the air. It's a nice change from the already cold weather in Chicago.

"Your mom accepting me back into her life never had anything to do with you. Sure, she was gentle with you, and didn't want to hurt you, but she doesn't need your permission to marry me."

"I know," I say sullenly.

"But you're acting like a toddler, putting her fingers in her ears and refusing to acknowledge or accept that it's going to happen regardless of whether you're onboard or not. Your mom wanted to delay the wedding, give you longer to accept it, but I told her hell no. I've waited long enough. Now imagine if I did to you what you're doing to me."

I rear my head back. He lifts the hood of the grill, and I'm happy to have his eyes off me for a second. "What does that mean?"

"If I told you I wasn't going to talk to you if you dated Miles. That I sure as hell wouldn't attend your wedding and told you the mistake you were making by marrying him."

"I never said those things." I move to stand.

"Your silence did. Your unwillingness to answer the phone did. Your inability to even discuss the wedding did."

"I'm sorry, okay? Jeez, I'm here now."

He turns around, crossing his arms.

"You want to know why I came here, Dad? To make peace with the fact that you were a womanizing asshole who left me in hotel rooms so he could search for some fresh pussy."

"Bryce!" My mom comes out of the kitchen, and my face heats.

My dad's gaze falls to the ground. "I made mistakes… a lot, I know that and I'm sorry for how they affected you. It's what you do when you realize you made the mistake that matters. I can't change the past, hell, I probably can't even make up for it. All I can do is move forward and be a better man." He puts the kabobs on the plate and turns off the grill. "Excuse me." He slides by my mom and me, going into the house.

My mom blows out a breath and picks up the plate, following him into the house and leaving me outside alone. I finish my beer, throw it in the recyclable trash can they leave outside, and go in to face the music.

"Mom," I say, entering the kitchen.

Her back is to me, and she raises her hand for me to stop. She turns around, and I'm not prepared to see her red-rimmed eyes and blotchy cheeks.

Guilt and pain well up inside me. "I—"

"No, Bryce. Sit down."

I sit at the kitchen table that's been set for dinner.

"I have chosen your dad," she says. "I know that is hard for you to hear, and neither one of us are proud of the things that transpired during the divorce. Parents have regrets because guess what? We've never done this before. Which you'll figure out for yourself as you continue to move through life, and hopefully have a husband and a family one day. It's all new, and mistakes will be made. He feels tremendous guilt for the person he was then. He thinks that he's responsible for your lack of trust in men, in love and relationships."

"Well… I mean…"

"Bryce…"

"I don't know what to do, Mom." My arms flail out to my sides. "I don't want to be like this. I don't. Do you think I don't want to open my arms to Miles and trust him completely? Of course I do. I hurt him so badly when I accused him of messing around on me. He's never going to forgive me." Tears burst from my eyes and my head falls into my hands.

"This is the real reason you came home. Not the job. The boy." She runs her hand over my back and hugs me into her side. "Oh, sweetie. Just let your wall down a little bit. He'll burst through it, or jump over it, or whatever it will take to have you."

"You've never met him. If you'd seen his face…" I hiccup through the tears.

"Your dad told me how he looks at you. He came home and said he thought we'd have a son-in-law joining the family soon."

I shake my head. "Talk about zero to sixty."

"Sometimes it's okay to go fast. Not everyone needs almost thirty years and a serious illness to make you realize your biggest regret."

I peek up, and she nods.

"I forgave your father, and I don't expect you to, but you will respect the relationship I have with him." She stares at me with those mom eyes. The ones where she's waiting for me to answer.

I nod.

"Good. Now I'm going to finish getting all this food out before it gets cold and you're going to go talk to your father. He's out the front on the swing."

"Mom…" I'm not even sure what I want to say.

She pats my knee. "The boy isn't gone. I promise you. But you need to deal with your dad before you go back to Miles. Your gut told you to come home because you know that's what you need to do." She puts her fingers over my heart. "It's the most powerful organ in your body. Listen to it." She stands and goes back over to the counter.

I wipe the tears from my face and let loose a shaky exhale.

After walking across my parents' expansive ranch bungalow, I open the front door and step outside. My dad is on the swing on the front porch, looking out at the neighborhood. I sluggishly walk over, and he slows the swing for me to get on, then rocks it back and forth again.

"I'm sorry," I say.

"No, you're not. And I'm okay with that." He glances at me. "If I could take it back, sweetie, I would've never divorced your mom. I would've been a better husband, a better father. But I was young and stupid and didn't want to take responsibility for my life." He shakes his head. "I didn't want to grow up. That's it. Plain and simple. But when I heard your mom got sick, my heart just fell to pieces." He cries, and I don't know what to do. I've never seen my dad so emotional. He struggles to catch his breath. "All the years I lost with her. It was like someone just cast a spell and I couldn't get here fast enough to help her through it. And your mom didn't take me back easily." He laughs. "You should know that. She made me work for it."

"I figured she would."

He laughs again and wipes his tears. "When she told me

she was giving me a second chance, I just… it was such a gift. I promise you, I'll never hurt her again. Ever."

I nod, my own tears spilling free. I haven't cried this much in years.

"But you… I wish I wasn't the one who made you so cynical of men. I was the first man in your life, and I failed you. I didn't set the example you needed growing up or show you how you should be treated. I could never be sorrier for anything in my life than that."

I lean my head on my dad's shoulder and we swing for a few minutes in silence. I'm not sure what to say. His admitting his mistakes doesn't make all the painful memories go away, but it does help, and I can see that this is the first step in healing.

Then I think of Miles. "I think I love him," I say, more tears cascading down my cheeks.

He places his hand over mine and squeezes. "So, go to him. Allow him to prove you wrong. Allow him to show you how a man should treat his woman."

We sit for a few more quiet seconds.

"Dad?"

"Yeah."

"I love you."

"Oh, sweetie, I love you so much." He wraps his arm around my shoulders, kissing the top of my head. "Thank you for coming home."

"Thank *you* for coming home. She's happy. Really happy."

"I hope so. Every day until I die is devoted to her."

He squeezes me tighter, and I hear the front door open.

"Okay, you bunch of crybabies. Dinner's ready." My mom comes over and my dad slows the swing so she can get on.

And we swing together, as a family, for the first time ever.

That wound that was so raw finally feels as though it's scabbing over.

CHAPTER 29
MILES

"I can't get her job back, Miles," Ronnie says with a sigh, tossing his apple in the trash can.

"You're buddies with Osterman. You can."

He blows out a breath. "We already have our people on the whole story this girl is spinning. You need to let it go. I feel bad for Bryce. I liked her, I did, but she knew the rules."

"So did I." I point at myself. "What's going to happen to me?"

He shrugs. Clearly he's never even thought about punishing me.

"A missed game?"

His eyebrows raise. "We're not going to bench our best player."

"But you'll switch his position?" He sighs, and I wave it off. I need to stop being a baby about that. "I cannot be the reason she loses her job. I cannot be the reason she isn't as far ahead in her career as she wants to be. It's everything to her."

"Why is this so important to you? It's just one woman."

I didn't want to go here and I sure as hell didn't want Ronnie Michaels to be the first to know, but if it helps Bryce, then that's what matters. "I love her."

His eyes widen, and he leans back in his chair. "Are you sure?"

I nod.

He studies me as though he thinks I'm lying.

"If you can't get her job back, I'm not going to be the player I am today. I'm going to be a nightmare of a PR problem, not to mention my hands might not be what they used to be. I might start missing those balls and find myself unable to track what direction my opponent's going in."

He smirks and clicks his tongue off the roof of his mouth. "Are you suggesting you're going to play like shit if I can't get her job back?"

"I'm just sayin'. Things happen. People change when the woman they love walks out on them."

He laughs, cackles really. "You give too much of a shit what fans think. You think I don't know you, Miles? You thrive off the attention you're getting now. You've always been the underdog, and this is finally your year. Fans can't get enough of you. You have more jersey sales than Cooper. You're trying to make me believe you'd give all that up for some girl you've been banging?"

"Absolutely. Football isn't who I am. It doesn't define me. She's my future. One day football will just be what I did. And on my tombstone, all I want it to say is MVP of my family."

He stares at me as though he's bored.

"I love her, Ronnie, and I'm going to do anything for her. If that means becoming the worst player in the league or the biggest head case, that's what I'll do. You can't change my mind."

He blows out a breath and stares out his window that overlooks the field. He stands and walks over, putting his hands in his pockets. "I'm not sure I understand players like you, Cavanaugh. Damon, I understand. This should be the time of your life." He turns to face me. "Women falling at your feet, sliding their numbers in your pockets. But you only want one woman and she's so important to you that you'd probably retire on the spot right now if you weren't contracted to the team for another year."

Absolutely, but I don't tell him that.

He shakes his head. "You have years in the future to be in a serious relationship. Why now, when you're a fucking icon?"

"I love her," I say again. "And I'm just not that guy. I'm a football player, not a player."

He walks back to his desk. "Let me see what I can do. She won't be able to write a word about you if I get her back here." He holds the receiver of his office phone but doesn't dial.

"Fine. I don't need that."

He continues to shake his head while he dials. I don't need him to understand what I'm doing; he just needs to do it.

When he's done dialing, he sits back in his seat. "Billy Boy. So, I've changed my mind. I'd like Bryce Burns back on the Grizzlies. She won't report a word about Cavanaugh though." He puts it on speakerphone and hangs up the receiver.

"I don't know, Ronnie. My rules were clear, and she broke them," Mr. Osterman says.

"She's way too talented for you to just give up on her. She covers the team but she can't report on him. We make that clear and the rest should be fine if she remains objective. I have no doubt she will."

There's silence on the other end.

"C'mon, you know she's better than Grant Thorn," Ronnie says.

"Why the change of mind?" he asks.

Ronnie looks at me and sighs. "She's starting out, and I feel bad?"

"And Miles Cavanaugh is sitting across from you right now, I gather?"

Ronnie laughs. "And he's quite the bargainer. So what do you say?"

"Jesus… okay."

"I'm the one who gets to tell her," I say, interrupting them.

"In other words, he wants to be her white knight," Ronnie says.

"Fine. But I need an answer by Monday because Grant is covering this week."

"I'll get you one. Thank you."

Ronnie hangs up with Mr. Osterman.

I stand and shake Ronnie's hand. When I go to pull away, he doesn't let go. "This is your one. Every player gets one free pass. This is yours. Don't ever bribe me or threaten me again with your playing performance or we'll have a serious problem."

"I won't. I promise."

He smiles and releases my hand.

As I walk out of the room, Damon hops off whoever's desk he's on. "So?"

"I got her job back. Now I just need her to give me a second chance."

"Wow, you must've been something in there," Damon says.

We take the elevator down and are about to leave the building when someone calls my name.

Tre Brummer waves and breaks the distance between us. His clothes are drenched in sweat, and he's wiping more sweat from his face. He's got a protein shake in his hand. "Hey, Miles."

"Tre."

He's so young. Was I that young when I joined the pros? I don't remember having that scared expression on my face.

"Can I talk to you for a second?"

Damon pats me on the back. "I'll get the Uber."

He leaves us alone, and Tre keeps his eyes on the ground,

then looks at me. "I just wanted to say sorry. I know you're probably pissed about the position shift, and I'm really working hard to get where they want me."

I smile at the kid. What seemed like life and death two days ago isn't so important now. And that's why Bryce means more than any of this shit.

"Don't sweat it, man. This is the pros. Things change a lot." I look out toward where Damon went. "I gotta go, but how about next practice, I show you some things that helped me when I started?"

"I'd love that." He looks around. "I feel a little out of my…"

"Scared as hell?"

He blows out a breath. "Yeah."

I laugh. "You're not alone." I put my hand out between us. "I've got you."

We do a slapping of hands and shake.

"Thanks. I thought for sure you were going to hate me."

"Ah… take it from me, Brummer, football isn't every-thing." I smile and turn around, rushing out of the stadium.

Damon's got the Uber already, the door open. "Set for the airport?"

"Yeah."

I slide in and he slides in next to me.

"Are you coming to Idaho with me?" I ask.

"No, but I got a friend who can help us out."

I scrunch my eyebrows.

"Get you on a plane," Damon adds.

"Go," I say to the Uber driver, and he speeds away.

CHAPTER 30

BRYCE

sit in Miles's apartment, waiting for him to return home. It's a little crazy how I had to get in. Cooper had Damon's key, and he had a key to Miles's place from when it was Creed's.

Now that I'm here, in Miles's space, I'm thinking maybe a call would've been better. I don't have any idea whether he'll be happy to see me. Maybe he'll be upset that I'm here alone in his private space.

There's the sound of a key in the door, and I hold my breath.

"I told you just to go to the airport. I don't need a bag." Miles is talking to someone.

"This is your first time meeting her mom. You can't show up like that. Put on some jeans and a nice button-down. I can't believe I have to dress you for the parents."

Damon.

"I don't think they'd care, and I don't think Bryce would either."

I cover my heart with my hand. He was going to go to Idaho for me. Hopefully that's a good sign.

"You can't take back a bad first impression."

"Who are you, and where is the real Damon?" Miles's voice draws closer, and I remain frozen, waiting to see him.

"I'm helping you, believe me."

"Have you seen my charger?" He finally appears in the family room and stops, blinking when he spots me. "Bryce?"

"And that's my cue." Damon winks at me and runs the other way. The door shuts a second later.

"Hey," I say. What I really want to do is run to him, jump in his arms, and beg him to take me back.

"I thought you were in Idaho?" He doesn't move closer, and I don't stand.

"I got back, like, an hour ago."

"Oh."

"I want to apologize," I say, wishing I would've rehearsed this on the plane. "It was wrong of me to accuse you. I know you wouldn't do that."

"Never," he says emphatically. "I would never." He shakes his head as if his words aren't enough.

"I just…" I sigh. This is harder to get out than I thought.

He rounds the sofa. "I understand. Your dad and the picture *was* incriminating. I was already mad that day because they were switching my position and I felt like a fucking failure. Not only in my career but with us. That I failed you if you thought I could ever do that. And I just didn't want to accept that." He sits on the chair across from me.

"You didn't fail me." Tears well in my eyes. "You were right, I was never all in. I think only part of my heart was open, but I can't stop crying now, so…" Tears spill down my face.

I fall to my knees and crawl over to him, then slide my hands up his legs. When he opens them, I crawl inside the space between his thighs.

"But I am now. I'm ready. A hundred and ten percent open to see where this goes."

"Your job," he says.

"I don't care. I quit. I can find another one. But there's only one you."

He bends and takes my face in his hands. "I got your job back. It's all yours."

"How? Why?" I shake my head. "I don't want it. If it means that I can't be with you, I don't want it. I just want you."

"You have me," he says. "I'm still all yours. You can't report on me, but that's okay."

"What do you mean?"

"You can report on the Grizzlies, just not this one. But it's your dream job. Take it back, Bryce. Please."

I place my hands over his on my cheeks. "No. I don't want it. That day they suspended me, I realized I wanted you way more than any job. You're my dream. Just you."

"You can have both now."

I smile. This man is too sweet. "They never liked the way I reported anyway. And I kind of like writing articles about you. Maybe I'll become your permanent PR person." He gives me a skeptical look, and I laugh. "I promise I'd be nice. So… do you forgive me?"

He nods. "I'll always forgive you. Well, within reason, but always."

"I was so stupid."

His thumbs wipe the tears from my eyes. "Stop it. It's over. Let's forget it and move forward." He stares into my eyes.

"Where do we go from here?" I practically whisper.

"How about I kiss you?"

"Please." I smile and nod.

He bends down and kisses my lips. He's gentle and sweet, and when he draws back, his eyes study me for a moment. "So, this was our first fight."

"It wasn't our first," I say, and he chuckles.

"Well, was it surprisingly horrible for you?"

"Very. But I'm really hoping the make-up sex is surprisingly hot."

He slides off the chair, and I inch backward, losing my balance and falling to my back.

"Oh, I'm gonna surprise you." He falls on me, and I wind my arms around his neck.

"I love you," I say.

His lips thin, and he stares at me as if he's mad.

"What?"

"I was going to say it first." He frowns.

I giggle. "I know, and I wanted to be first."

Miles rolls his eyes. "Of course, I should've known."

"But you can say it now?"

He shakes his head.

"Come on. Say it."

"Nope." He grins.

"Miles." My hands rest on his cheeks now. "Say it."

"You can't make me," he says, and I wiggle to get out from under him. "Where are you going?"

"If you're not gonna—"

He catches me and lies back on top of me. He looks into my eyes, and I take in his beautiful blues. He doesn't have to say a word, it's all there, but that doesn't stop him. "I love you, Bryce Burns."

"I know."

He shakes his head again and I pull it down to mine, sealing it with a kiss.

EPILOGUE
MILES

THE BIG GAME

Bryce opens the hotel curtains first thing in the morning. "Today is the day!"

I hate how she's so chipper in the morning, but at the same time, morning sex is awesome with her since she's not half asleep.

"I can't believe we're here," I say.

She jumps on the bed. "And you're going to make MVP today."

I grab her waist and pull her down onto me. "Trying to put good things out into the universe again?"

She laughs. "No. My man is going to play the game of his life today and come home with the award."

"It doesn't matter. The fact that I get to wake up to you is what my dreams are made of."

She rolls her eyes and pushes off my chest. "You say the sweetest things, but you want that title. That trophy."

It would be nice, but these past months with Bryce have just confirmed she's the right choice, hands down. She's my number one in my life.

I go to the bathroom, and I hear her typing on her laptop. She's probably been up for hours before me.

"Still working on that thing?" I ask.

She decided to write her own piece on the Chicago Grizzlies and publish it in the new magazine she's working at, which is *Sportsverse's* biggest competitor.

The woman who took a picture on my bed came forward right after Bryce and I got back together—after she found out that Bryce had lost her job. She told us that Shelly had paid her to do it and given her the key to my place. I thought about pressing charges, but she seemed genuinely sorry for her actions, so I didn't.

How did Shelly have a key to my apartment? From when it was Creed's. Turns out Shelly and Creed were seeing each other in secret and the baby is his. When he said it wasn't and refused a relationship with the child as well as any responsibility, she wanted revenge. Yeah, I guess she could've just sued him or something but she was afraid to lose her job, so she opted to hide the pregnancy, hoping she could convince Creed to step up.

After Grant Thorn told Shelly how he saw us together at the planetarium, she saw it as an opportunity to sell her story and make a lot of money. All while screwing us over.

"Just adding the finishing touches. Just so you know, in the last part, I'm writing how you're winning the MVP and the Grizzlies win the Bowl." She types away, smiling.

"I appreciate the faith."

She sets down her computer and crosses the room in her small silk pajama set. "Because tonight I need to be with you, celebrating your big win." She rises on her tiptoes and kisses me. "Love you."

"The whole crew here?" I ask.

"Yeah, I'll see them in the box."

"All right. I'm taking a shower."

Bryce goes back to her article, and I turn on the shower. As the spray washes down on me, I can't help but feel so damn lucky to have her. We're going to move in together. She actually agreed to move into The Den, and we hope that having a woman there will change the reputation of the place. We really need Damon to change to help with that effort.

A couple hours later, we head over to the game and Bryce kisses me goodbye, going to the box while I head to the locker room. The nerves are real. I'm fucking scared.

Pavin returned to strong safety only three weeks ago, and I got my free safety position back. I felt bad for Tre, but he'll get his chance. He made incredible plays in those three weeks. So many I was a little scared, but only because I want to play to support the life I want with Bryce, not for my ego.

Cooper sits down next to me on the bench.

"You good?" I ask.

He nods. "It's a lot of pressure. All eyes on us."

"And we're going to win. Bryce put it out in the universe this morning."

He laughs. "I'm not sure which Bryce I prefer, the old one or this new Zen one, but she's really changed. She's so optimistic."

"Yeah, she is."

"Congratulations, man, you guys seem really happy."

"We are."

"Wedding bells?" His eyebrows rise.

I look around to see if anyone is paying us any attention, then I look back at Cooper. "Her parents are getting married in a few months. I'm going to let her get through that first and then maybe. I gotta watch how fast I go with her. You know how she is."

He doesn't say anything, but he doesn't have the chance to because Damon jumps in front of us. "Let's go!"

Coach Iverson comes out of the office and gives us an inspirational speech about our season and how it all comes down to one game, but this doesn't define us. He's proud of our hard work this season. It's what got us here. "You boys have all the tools to go out there and play the toughest sixty minutes of your lives and come home as champions."

By the end, we're all psyched and run out of the locker room, down the tunnel, and onto the field as the announcers say our names in the big stadium.

I barely remember the majority of the game. We were down, then up. I deflected two passes and grabbed another one to return it forty yards. I swear I heard Bryce over everyone in the stadium, cheering on that play. I'm not sure about the MVP though. Cooper had a great game, fast out of the pocket and Damon had rushing yards plus he caught and ran in for two touchdown passes.

For the final play of the game, I get in front of the wide receiver, jumping, reaching, and catching the ball to stop our opponents from tying the game. That might have been the best moment of my career.

When the clock runs out, orange and blue confetti floats down from above and all our families rush onto the field. There are hugs and people congratulating us, and Coach Iverson takes me in his arms and says things a father would.

Chase made Twyla stay in the booth with Brady and Violet and Theo because they're both pregnant and they'll get jostled down on the field, but my parents come down with Lee and Shayna. I hear Bryce coming when she screams my name and runs toward me. I pick her up and swing her around.

"I told you!" she screams over all the noise. "It's yours, I knew it."

I lower her to the ground and kiss her. "Thank you for being my number one fan."

She smiles, then takes my head in her hands and rises on her tiptoes.

Then I'm rushed over to the stage, but I grab Bryce's hand because she's going to be there with me if I win this award.

First, Ollie Pradham calls Ronnie, Coach Iverson, and our owner, Dan Towers, to the stage. All us players linger in the background and wait. Cooper and Damon are right there with me. Damon has his phone out, taking pictures of all the action until he stops abruptly, and his eyes widen on his phone.

"What?" I mouth to him, but he waves me off.

After a large bout of cheers, Ollie talks again. "And our Most Valuable Player! This individual hasn't only had an incredible season, but he had one helluva game tonight. I think I speak for us all when I say it was amazing watching him perform this season, in not one but two different positions. He's a true inspiration and an incredible athlete. The MVP award goes to…" The crowd goes crazy. "Miles Cavanaugh!"

Bryce jumps into my arms, kissing my entire face. "Congratulations!"

My body feels a little numb as I walk up and accept the award from Ronnie. Dan Towers passed it to him—probably because Ronnie is the one who traded for me. Ollie hands me the microphone.

"This is for Chicago. Thank you for trusting me to come back this year and prove my worth to you. Some of you were skeptical, I know, but let me introduce you to the woman who has always pushed me the hardest. She's the love of my life, and this isn't just for me but for her too. Baby"—I look at Bryce with the award high in my hand—"you put it out into the universe, and it came true. I love you for believing in me. My life would be nothing without you."

She wraps her arms around me, and I bend down to kiss her. The stadium roars to life.

We step down from the platform, and the other Grizzlies congratulate me, but Damon isn't there. I find him later, sitting in an empty chair by the tunnel. When I walk over, he looks at me, his face not reflecting the joy of someone who just won the championship.

"What's going on?" I ask.

He stands and whispers in my ear, "Remember that girl from the rooftop the day you moved in?"

I nod.

"She's pregnant and says the baby is mine."

I draw back with wide eyes. I've never seen Damon so upset. Talk about life taking a one-eighty.

Time for Peter Pan to grow up.

The End

COCKAMAMIE
UNICORN RAMBLINGS

And you thought we weren't going to give you Miles and Bryce's book?!?

We understand the confusion but rest assured we'd never do that to you. If we tease out a couple a lot, know that you'll always get the couple, we just can't promise when.

Originally, Miles' story was supposed to be the fourth book in the Kingsmen Football Stars series, but we felt like we didn't set up our characters for books five and six well enough to finish out the series in San Francisco. We chatted and decided that Miles and Bryce's story would be the perfect start to a new football series and that is how SOMETHING LIKE HATE came to be. When we were deciding who our Chicago Grizzlies would be we thought it would be a great opportunity to bring Damon Siska back from False Start and add Cooper Rice as quarterback, because who doesn't love a quarterback?!?

By trading Miles, we knew we had to get Bryce to Chicago, too. Their storyline changed a lot from plotting to execution, even while we were writing. At one point toward the end, as Rayne wrote the first draft, Piper was right behind her revising and the story changing in real time with messages back and forth between the two of us. This was a big change for us to be working on something this closely while the rough draft was being written. We actually loved it and hope to do more of our stories that way. Of course, it only happened that way because Rayne is the biggest procrastinator on Earth. LOL

We hope you loved the addition of Cooper and Ellery, and the return of Damon Siska… yes, we know he needs redeeming. That's something we *love* to do with our characters, and we promise you're going to love him by the time his book ends.

As always, we have a lot of people to thank for getting this book into your hands!

Nina and the entire Valentine PR team.
Cassie from Joy Editing for line edits.
Ellie from My Brother's Editor for line edits.
Rachel from My Brother's Editor for proofreading.
Hang Le for the cover and branding for the entire series.
All the bloggers who read, review, share and/or promote us.
The Piper Rayne Unicorns in our Facebook group who are our biggest cheerleaders!
Every reader who took the time to read this book! Thank you for granting us your most precious resource—time. We don't take that lightly.

Next up is Damon Siska… yeah, he's a bachelor and a playboy, but those make the best surprise baby daddies, don't they?

xo,
Piper & Rayne

ABOUT PIPER & RAYNE

Piper Rayne is a USA Today Bestselling Author duo who write "heartwarming humor with a side of sizzle" about families, whether that be blood or found. They both have e-readers full of one-clickable books, they're married to husbands who drive them to drink, and they're both chauffeurs to their kids. Most of all, they love hot heroes and quirky heroines who make them laugh, and they hope you do, too!

ALSO BY PIPER RAYNE

Chicago Grizzlies

On the Defense (Free Prequel)

Something like Hate

Something like Lust

Something like Love

The Nest

Mr. Heartbreaker

Mr. Broody

Mr. S (Title to be revealed)

Mr. C (Title to be revealed)

Kingsmen Football Stars

False Start (Free Prequel)

You Had Your Chance, Lee Burrows

You Can't Kiss the Nanny, Brady Banks

Over My Brother's Dead Body, Chase Andrews

Plain Daisy Ranch

One Last Summer

The One I Left Behind

The One I Stood Beside

The One I Didn't See Coming

The Baileys

Lessons from a One-Night Stand (FREE)

Advice from a Jilted Bride

Birth of a Baby Daddy

Operation Bailey Wedding (Novella)

Falling for My Brother's Best Friend

Demise of a Self-Centered Playboy

Confessions of a Naughty Nanny

Operation Bailey Babies (Novella)

Secrets of the World's Worst Matchmaker

Winning my Best Friend's Girl

Rules for Dating Your Ex

Operation Bailey Birthday (Novella)

The Greene Family

My Twist of Fortune (Free Prequel)

My Beautiful Neighbor (FREE)

My Almost Ex

My Vegas Groom

A Greene Family Summer Bash (Novella)

My Sister's Flirty Friend

My Unexpected Surprise

My Famous Frenemy

A Greene Family Vacation (Novella)

My Scorned Best Friend

My Fake Fiancé

My Brother's Forbidden Friend

A Greene Family Christmas (Novella)

Lake Starlight

The Problem with Second Chances

The Issue with Bad Boy Roommates

The Trouble with Runaway Brides

The Drawback of Single Dads

Modern Love

Charmed by the Bartender

Hooked by the Boxer

Mad about the Banker

Single Dads Club

Real Deal

Dirty Talker

Sexy Beast

Hollywood Hearts

Mister Mom

Animal Attraction

Domestic Bliss

Bedroom Games

Cold as Ice

On Thin Ice

Break the Ice

Chicago Law

Smitten with the Best Man

Tempted by my Ex-Husband

Seduced by my Ex's Divorce Attorney

Blue Collar Brothers

Flirting with Fire

Crushing on the Cop

Engaged to the EMT

White Collar Brothers

Sexy Filthy Boss

Dirty Flirty Enemy

Wild Steamy Hook-up

The Rooftop Crew

My Bestie's Ex

A Royal Mistake

The Rival Roomies

Our Star-Crossed Kiss

The Do-Over

A Co-Workers Crush

Hockey Hotties

Countdown to a Kiss (Free Prequel)

My Lucky #13 (FREE)

The Trouble with #9

Faking it with #41

Tropical Hat Trick (Novella)

Sneaking around with #34

Second Shot with #76

Offside with #55

Holiday Romances

Single and Ready to Jingle

Claus and Effect

Merry Kissmas